A HISTORY OF MY WEIRD

CHLOË HEUCH

First published in 2024
by Firefly Press
25 Gabalfa Road, Llandaff North, Cardiff, CF14 2JJ
www.fireflypress.co.uk

A CIP catalogue record of this book is available from the British Library.

ISBN 978-1-915444-63-9
ebook ISBN ISBN 978-1-915444-64-6

This book has been published with the support of the Books Council Wales.

Typeset by Elaine Sharples

Printed and bound by CPI Group (UK) Ltd,
Croydon, Surrey, CRO 4YY

For Dylan and Rose.

TUESDAY 7 SEPTEMBER

Don't move feet, don't move. I'm sitting in my science classroom, in the uncomfortable seats, trying to stop my feet from twitching.

Mr Jones is going on about food chains to my new class, 7D. I learnt all this stuff in primary so I'm mainly concentrating on my feet and trying not to stim. I explained stimming to Maya once. It's something I can't help. Stimming makes me feel a bit calmer or happier. But she just said it was weird and if I wanted to be friends with her, I should stop.

My new class has a mix of kids from our old primary school and other primaries too. Mr Jones has let everyone sit where they like today as it is the first day. I wanted to sit with Ellie and Maya, but the tables are in rows and only have space for two. They are stuck together, as usual, so I sat behind them. On my own. I look around the class at all the new people. Loads of names I don't know yet. Loads of people who I have got to try to understand. The thought of it exhausts me.

Then Mr Jones starts talking about predators. He mentions sharks. I love anything to do with the sea, so I start to listen. He shows us a clip from a film where a megalodon is about to bite someone in half: a megalodon, *not* a shark.

Ellie puts her hand up. 'My uncle lives in Australia. There are loads of shark attacks there.'

Another kid I don't know says, 'I've seen that film – the giant shark eats the whole village one by one!'

Most of the class start talking about it excitedly, apart from a couple of children on the edges of the room who are sat on their own like me, not speaking. One is a kid with black hair cut to her shoulders. I notice she is wearing earrings with dangly moons. It makes me feel a tiny bit better that I'm not the only person on my own; a tiny bit braver for what I'm about to do.

Mr Jones smiles. 'Yes, sharks do capture our imagination as nightmares from the deep…'

I hate speaking in class. I only speak if it's important … but I know this stuff is wrong! Sharks get such bad press and I *have* to tell them — even though it feels like someone is trampolining about on my insides.

So I say, 'That isn't a shark. It's a megalodon – they've been extinct for over three million years.'

'Oh right, we've got a know-it-all.' Mr Jones sighs dramatically. He checks the class register and glances at me. 'Next time you want to speak, put your hand up, young lady.'

I put my hand up, like he asks, and carry on talking. 'It's Mo, sir. And sharks aren't really dangerous. For your information, there are only five shark attacks on humans per year whereas humans kill millions of sharks every year.'

Mr Jones folds his arms. 'True, but I think we can all agree that *some* sharks are *very* dangerous.' He smiles at the class and nods.

Ellie flicks her ponytail round and glares at me mouthing, '*Shut up*'.

But I can't. My hand waves about above my head like a flag in a storm.

'Mr Jones, I think you should clarify *very*. You stand a greater risk of being killed by lightning or in a car accident.'

Ellie, Maya and the rest of the class have stopped talking and turned to stare at me. I try not to think about them, but about how important it is they know the truth. I can't believe our teacher doesn't know this! I'm sure he'll thank me for setting him straight.

Mr Jones walks around his desk and fiddles with the remote for the whiteboard. I take this as a sign he is listening, so I carry on. 'Shark populations are decreasing across the planet and some are critically endangered. The demand for shark fin soup, for example, has led to millions being caught. Their fins are ripped from their bodies—'

'Mo…' Mr Jones' hands are on his hips. Some of the other kids are whispering now.

'—and they are thrown back into the water only to drown. It is truly barbaric.' I hear *weird* and *why doesn't she just shut up?* But I can't stop. 'You should be educating people about what beautiful creatures sharks are instead of feeding the false myths about them—'

'Mo!' Mr Jones face is going red and shiny. He looks like a cross giraffe.

'—instead of scaring people saying sharks are dangerous, you should spend your time telling students that driving to school is dangerous, or … or crossing the road—'

SMACK! Mr Jones hits the desk with his palm. 'OUTSIDE NOW!'

I blink at him. This does not sound like he's grateful. I don't know why I bother! THIS is why I don't do people. I never understand them.

'NOW!' he repeats.

I walk out of the room stunned. What have I done

wrong? Why isn't Mr Jones pleased I was able to set him straight and stop him lying to the class? My insides fall into my feet, leaving an empty gnawing gap. I don't understand why he overreacted! I'm so rubbish at life.

I'm still standing outside the door a few moments later when the class pours out for break. One kid whispers 'Loser' when he goes past, but the kid with black hair and dangly moon earrings pauses in front of me. She thrusts a piece of scrunched-up paper into my hand and gives me a thumbs-up.

I open the note. There is an awesome picture of a shark with someone in its mouth, who looks a bit like Mr Jones. I snort with laughter and look up to say thanks, but she is disappearing down the corridor in a tide of moving bodies.

'Mo, next time, can you keep your opinions to yourself?' Ellie stops in front of me so I stuff the note into my coat pocket. She's flanked on either side by Maya and another girl I don't know. They all look the same – high ponytail, high eyebrows, their arms are folded making a barrier of crosses. 'Mr Jones won't show us the film now, because of *you.* He says some people are *too sensitive.* He said he *was* going to let us watch it all next lesson, but *now* we have to do an essay instead.'

'So? I'm glad we don't have to watch the stupid film. It's a load of crud.' I cross my arms too.

They all crowd round me, in my space. My skin prickles like electrocuted jelly. My brain feels too full. I want to go home and crawl into bed under the duvet away from all these 'pick-me' girls and idiot teachers.

'Just 'cause you wanted to show off. You have no idea about secondary school. You're just so *embarrassing*,' Maya says.

'No.' I close my eyes for a moment. A headache's coming. 'Just 'cause you're too stupid.'

'*Sharks don't bite at all! They're vegetarian!*' Another look-alike girl mimics. They all cackle and someone bumps into me, pushing an elbow into my arm.

'Get off me!' I blink my eyes open, bringing up my arm to protect myself, propelling Ellie away. She over-balances, topples backwards into the others, trips and falls.

Just at that moment Mr Jones opens his door. Typical.

'Sir, Mo just really hurt Ellie.' They crowd round Ellie on the floor, helping her to her feet.

'No, I didn't! I—'

'I've had enough of you, Mo! Get to the head's office and out of my sight!'

WEDNESDAY 8 SEPTEMBER

'Detention already?' Diane, my step-mum, asks.

I ignore her question and sit down for breakfast.

'You need to learn to be quiet in class, Mo,' she says, mashing some banana into a bowl.

Stink (aka Ewan, my baby brother) bangs his spoon and blows a raspberry at her. Exactly what I'm thinking.

'Teachers hate being shown up – they'll always make an example of you.'

'But he was wrong!' I splash milk into my bowl. 'It's not fair.'

Diane looks at me sympathetically. 'It will get better. It's only your first week.'

I stir the Wheetie O shapes, poke them and try to drown them in milk. I can't imagine 'it' getting any better. All my classes have been rubbish so far, but science was the worst. The kid who gave me the note wasn't sat anywhere near me after that and I am rubbish at all that socialising stuff. Ellie and Maya are being mean and no one else talked to me. I think if secondary school is still this bad next week I'm going to run away to the woods and forage for my food. I could make a little house out of sticks.

'Mah?' Stink flicks his spoon in my direction and grins at me. I dodge the flecks of banana goop that spray across the kitchen table.

Diane comes behind my stool and gives me a hug. She smells of sticky banana and jasmine shower gel. 'Remember, we're going to go to Blue Zoo as a treat – just ten more sleeps.'

'Bribery,' I mutter, but not too loud, because I really want to go to Blue Zoo. They have piranhas.

'Ready for school?' Dad asks, walking into the kitchen.

'Mo's got a lunchtime detention.' Diane shows Dad the email.

'Disruptive behaviour?' Dad raises his eyebrows in disbelief at me.

I shrug and chew my Wheetie Os slowly.

'The school will know Mo's autistic, won't they?' he asks Diane.

'Bound to,' Diane says, piling another spoonful of banana goop for Stink. 'The primary school will have sent all the info. And anyway, I'm sure Ffion is all over it.'

'What about mum?' I say, hearing her name.

'Diane just means your mum is bound to sort it. Don't worry.' He ruffles my hair.

'We all know you're not disruptive, are you, Mo? You're clever and unique.' He checks his watch. 'Got your bag? Phone?' He puts his arms around me and gives me a squish, too. 'What's your timetable for today?'

I get my planner out of my bag and look in the back. I scan through. History, sigh. Science, double sigh. 'I think I'm getting a fever and you need to let me stay off.'

'Fat chance,' Dad says reading over my shoulder. 'You've got HWE in the afternoon.'

'What is *that*?'

'Hippos, Whales and Elephants. You'll get to learn all about how to be a hippo, then how it feels to be a whale… Oww!' Dad pretends to nurse his arm where I slapped it away.

'Didn't your parents ever tell you it's rude to hit people?'

'Shut UP, Dad!' I put the planner back in my bag and zip it up.

'Health and Wellbeing Education,' Diane says, being the sensible one as usual.

'Dah!' Stink says, grinning and waving his arms about.

'Come on then, Mo.' Dad takes my hand and pulls me off the chair to a standing position. 'It's time to go.'

'See you next week.' Diane catches me for a last hug as I walk past.

'Gah!' Stink explains. He smells sweet today and not of poo, which is nice. There's still quite a lot of banana on his cheeks and some globs in his hair. He holds out the spoon in his fat little banana-encrusted hand and waves it at me. He is way too sticky to touch. So, I boop his nose instead.

'Mum's this weekend then. I'll see you on Wednesday, okay?' Dad pulls up and waits for me to climb out of the van. I watch other kids walking slowly up the school drive, and up the steps into the mouth of the building. I wonder how bad it will be today.

I'm lining up for registration and the kid who gave me the shark note appears behind me. I'm just about to say thank you and tell her I loved her drawing when Ellie barges into the queue behind me and the girl is pushed to the back. I make it my mission to say something to her by the end of the day.

I avoid any trouble in the morning by simply not talking. At all. For my lunchtime detention I have to go and sit in a classroom with some other kids, all from other year groups. It's really boring and means I hardly have any time to eat my lunch and no time at all to try to speak to the note-giving kid.

At the end Mr Gross, the deputy head, says to me that he understands I'm autistic and I might not be able to manage my feelings but that I'm going to have to learn. It's a good job I'm still so cross about the unfairness of it; it stops me feeling upset. Eventually it's the afternoon and it is time to find out what HWE is really all about.

'Come in! Come in!' The HWE teacher is dressed in a bright orange shirt with a sun on it. I see a tattoo peeking out of the edge of her collar. She's smiling – a teacher actually smiling! That's a first for secondary school. I was coming to the conclusion that it must be part of their training: YOU MUST NOT SMILE.

She doesn't have a seating plan – we are allowed to sit with whoever we want. I spot Ellie and Maya and hesitate, wondering whether I should try and sit near them. At least I'd have someone to talk to. But Ellie turns her back on me and starts whispering to one of the wannabes hanging around her and Maya. They all start giggling and looking at me. I wonder if Ellie and Maya are going to be this horrid when we are back in gymnastics on Friday or if they will stop being so mean. I decide to keep away from them and I head to the back. There is one desk with a space free, next to the kid from science class who gave me the note! She doesn't look at me, so I assume it's okay for me to sit down. I put my coat on the back of the chair and wonder if I should say thank you now or—

'Welcome!' The weird smiley teacher beams. 'So, you're 7D.' She pauses a minute as she looks about the class. It's as though she is drinking us all in. 'My name is Ms Latimer.'

'Miss,' Ellie says, putting her hand up and speaking at the same time – like I was told I *must not* do. 'What is Ms, miss?'

'And you are?' Ms Latimer looks down at a paper in her hand. 'Ah, Ellie!'

Ellie nods, smoothing away an imaginary wisp of hair into her perfect ponytail.

'Ms – well, does anyone know what Ms stands for?' Ms Latimer looks about.

I avoid her gaze. I know it stands for someone who isn't married or doesn't want people to know whether they are married, but I don't say anything. One thing I've learnt at secondary school: *I must not show that I know things.*

'Men just have Mr, don't they?' The class nods. 'So, people don't know if they are married or not. It's private information. Women have traditionally had two titles that show whether they are unmarried, Miss, or if they are married, Mrs. Ms is fairer. That's why I like it. But I won't get cross if you accidentally call me Miss.' Ms Latimer grins. 'Right, what is HWE?'

She starts to discuss what it means. (Dad was so wrong – surprise. Diane was right.) And we haven't even done the register!

'Okay, I need some volunteers.' Ms Latimer grins.

Loads of hands shoot up. Mine stays firmly by my side. I don't understand why kids do that – volunteer for something when you don't even know what it is! *Hey, child, you have volunteered to jump off the roof. You have volunteered for extra maths after school for the rest of the year.*

Ms Latimer picks a few people and – *surprise*! – Ellie's one of them. The volunteers get to do drama at the front of the class. Ellie is the teacher and she has to teach the other kids. They are being deliberately difficult. Ellie ends up shouting they are all in after-school detention – yes, she does have a sly look in my direction. Ms Latimer asks people to put their hands up to talk about Ellie's good leadership qualities. (Errr…) And then we have to do a spider diagram about what makes a good leader.

I think about Mr Jones. He's a rubbish leader. He's made me hate my favourite subject. I think about my gymnastics coach. I've not seen her since before the holidays. She's okay, but I don't think I would describe her as good.

My spider diagram is empty and Ms Latimer's walking up the rows looking at people's work. I'm going to get yet another telling off.

Think. THINK! Leadership. Leeeeeeead.

'Hey, you must be Maureen.' Ms Latimer is by my desk. A waft of coffee, lavender and mint billows about her.

'I prefer Mo.'

'Okay. Cool. I'll just make a note – Mo. How are you doing with this? Any ideas?' she asks. I am looking at her silver bracelets. She has loads of them all falling over each other.

I move my hand to show her my empty mind map.

'Not got any ideas?'

'I can think of what isn't good leadership,' I mutter, twiddling my pen.

'So, what isn't good?'

I shrug. 'Making people feel bad?'

'Oh yes, brilliant. If a leader makes people feel bad, those people aren't going to want to do what the leader asks, are they?'

I shake my head and raise my eyes from my pen. Ms Latimer's lanyard is covered in badges: a Shakespeare quote, a Harry Potter badge, a hedgehog…

'So, what is the opposite of that?'

I shrug again. 'Making people feel good?'

'Yes! Exactly. So how do leaders do that? What do you think – Carys?' Ms Latimer directs this to the curtain of black hair that is sat next to me. Carys shakes her head. 'Why don't you two help each other think about what leaders can do to motivate and inspire others?' Ms Latimer grins at me again, and I let my eyes meet hers just for a moment. Her smile is even in her eyes. She begins to walk down the next row talking to each student as she goes.

'You got anything?' I ask Carys.

'Nope.' She shakes her fringe and shows me her blank page. 'No teachers here are any good. I can't think.'

'She's okay.' I nod at Ms Latimer.

Carys' mouth twists a little.

'Well, at least she smiles,' I say.

'Let's put friendly.' Carys writes it on her mind map in even scrawlier writing than mine.

'Yeah. And kind. Better than all the other teachers at Ysgol *Awfu…l*.'

She smirks. 'Like what you've done there – Ysgol *Offa…l*.'

The lesson goes fast. Carys and I end up thinking of loads of ideas, including giving kids sweets and extra lie-ins, and I decide Hippos, Whales and Elephants isn't so bad. We are packing up when I finally get the courage to say it.

'Thanks for the shark drawing. You're a really good artist.'

Carys shrugs and puts her head on one side. 'I like art. I thought the teacher was really stupid that lesson.'

I'm just about to reply when Ms Latimer gets everyone to listen.

'Before I forget. Even though I'm here teaching you HWE, my main subject is drama! You don't get to do much drama in year seven – though we do a bit in HWE. You do, however, get to come to my lunchtime club. It starts next week: Tuesdays and Fridays in the drama studio. Come along. We even have biscuits.'

I catch a glance from Carys and she grins at me as we file out of the classroom.

I trudge out after everyone else. I have English next. It isn't until I'm lining up outside the door that I realise Carys Curtain Hair is beside my elbow.

'You gonna go to drama club?' the hair asks.

'Maybe. You?'

She shrugs. 'I will if you will.'

'Okay.' I smile at her. I think I've made a friend!

FRIDAY 10 SEPTEMBER

I pull myself up onto the bar, stomach against the wood, hands in the correct position, then I twist round and jump down to finish. I feel hot as a baked potato and out of breath – and I've only been round the equipment twice! I pause for a moment, hands on my hips, watching the other gymnasts. Everyone else is on the mats now doing jumps and turns. They all look better than me, copies of each other – skinny and small as birds. That's what I looked like before the summer; before I had my growth spurt and I shot up like an overexcited sunflower; before *everything* started to change.

Coach blows her whistle and we come running. She waits a moment for us to gather round. Maya, Ellie, Sally, Tamzin and Nina look like five neat robins in a row, slim legs balanced, hair pulled tight into buns. And there's me on the end, like some giant gangly crow.

'Goodness, Mo. What did they feed you in Cornwall? You're almost as tall as me!' Coach says.

The robins laugh and preen. Ellie whispers something to Maya, who sniggers. Have they always been like this with me? When I'm winning at something, they are nice, but the rest of the time… I can't believe I've never really seen it before.

I shrug my shoulders and my smile slides off my face. I feel all their critical gazes. Ellie and Maya haven't spoken to me since the incident at school. I thought it might be better here at gymnastics, that it would go back to normal, but no.

'Right then,' says Coach. 'We need to talk about the competition next week. Floor first then: Tamzin – you're doing hoop; Ribbons – Sally; Acro – Ellie and Maya. And vault…' She pauses and glances at me before turning her gaze to Nina. 'As you've missed a few weeks, Mo, I'm going to let Nina do vault and trampoline in the local. We can reassess before the regionals, okay?'

'But I always do vault,' I say. I'm the best at vault.

'Get yourself back up to speed and, like I say, we'll think again about the regionals.'

'But I always—'

'See you next week,' she says, turning away from me.

Voices chorus around me as the others flit to the edge of the gymnasium to collect bags and water bottles.

'Coach,' I say to get her attention. 'I always do vault.'

'Well, it won't hurt to change things about a bit. I'm not saying you are off the team.' She crosses her arms. 'But I have heard there's been a bit of nastiness at school. Ellie's mum told me she hurt her arm because you pushed her. I think we need a harmonious team at the moment.'

I feel a rush of heat billow upwards through my body. The injustice of it! 'It wasn't my fau—'

Coach puts her hand up in front of me, like a stop sign. 'We can see how everyone is getting on next week. Okay? Regionals are a while off yet. Now, go. Your mum will be waiting.' She turns her back on me and walks over to the other coach.

'Never mind, Mo.' Ellie is next to me, her hand perched on her skinny hip. 'Maybe you'll remember to keep your temper now.'

'Or just keep away from us,' Maya says, touching away an imaginary hair from her face.

'You're ... you're so mean.' I push past them, grabbing my shoes in one hand and my water in the other. I can't believe how nasty they are being to me. Have they always been like this? How could I have missed it? And what do I do now?

'Okay, Mo?' Mum is waiting in reception with

all the other parents. The little ones are tripping and jumping about the room, waiting for their turn on the equipment, all excited. I want to tell them: don't bother.

Mum's face drops its smile. 'Mo, shoes?'

But I can't stop to talk. It's too much. Ellie. Maya. No competition. Secondary school. I have to get out of here, out into the cool air. My bare feet register the cold sharp gravel as I hurry to the car.

'What's wrong?' Mum tries when we are safe in our seats. 'Is it Coach? The comp?'

'I'm not in it.'

'Oh. Did Coach say why?'

'My fitness levels. Oh yeah, and I need to lose a foot in height. And—'

I'm about to mention Ellie, but Mum starts talking.

'Oh, Mo. Don't be sad.' I can hear the sadness between *her* words like she is filling up with my feelings. That makes me angrier. 'We thought this might happen, didn't we? Because of being off with the cough, and then the holiday. Don't stress,' she says, reassuring herself as she eases the car out of the car park. 'We can get you back to full fitness again. And there are loads of tall gymnasts. Marie Hindermann. That Russian one … ooh, I can't remember her name now—'

'It's not just that!' I shout, hiding my face in the crook of my arm. My head is too full to explain. It is like a chubby wet cloud has taken up residence there. I am never going back. Everything is changing, everything is different and I am done with all this. All this effort I've been putting in since I was four. I'm done.

She pauses for a few moments, then more quietly she says, 'I'll give Coach a ring and chat to her about how you feel – about the tall thing. I'm sure she can put your mind at rest.'

'No point. I'm never doing gymnastics again.'

As soon as I'm home I head for the bathroom. I slam the door shut and yank off my stupid red costume. Water gushes into the bath. I throw a mix of bubble bath into the stream, watching as the liquid froths into white. Then as soon as it is hot enough, I clamber in while it fills around me. The sound of the running water and the reflections on the surface immediately help me calm down. I let my head bob back and feel my hair soak with warmth.

'Mo.' The bathroom door handle turns.

'Mum! I'm having a bath!' I call crossly.

'Oh right.' I can hear the sigh in Mum's voice like a fat toad sitting on the words. 'Are you okay?'

I don't answer.

'Aw, MoMo. Don't give up just yet. I've spoken to Coach – she didn't mean you were too tall...'

I put my fingers in my ears and dip under the water. I can still hear her voice but the words blend together, the warm bubbles bobbing against my ears. I can feel the thrum of sound through the water. Is this how whales feel when boats go past? Engines thrumming like voices in the sea.

I used to love gymnastics – it was my SI (special interest) or *obsession* as Dad called it. I had a bar in my room and I'd hang like a bat for ages. I'd even read like that sometimes. I was in the development team in my club and went three times a week. I've been to competitions over the last couple of years and I've won two silvers and two golds for bar and vault.

Ellie and Maya used to be nice to me, too, when I was winning things. I've always been different from them but it didn't seem to matter. Now they are like one person with two heads always agreeing with each other and looking at me as though I am a person made of stinky cheese.

My body feels different too – lumpy and oversized. I don't want to put the smooth shimmering suits on. I used to love performing my routines; how easily my body worked for me and how I could make every move perfect. Not anymore. I hate people looking at me. It's like, all of a sudden I'm wearing my difference on my skin and everyone can see.

It hasn't helped that six months ago the 'spider legs' started and changed everything.

I'd first noticed them then: a single sinister hair on my skin that wouldn't brush away. Now there is a small army of pubic hairs. They make me think of spiders, as though arachnids are marching under my skin, their legs sticking through — horrible wiggly ugly things that are ruining everything. I pull at a pube and watch as it makes my skin tent upwards. There is no chance of pulling them out, they are as strong as wires.

The thrumming of Mum's voice has stopped. I turn the taps off and close my eyes. I let my arms and head float and imagine my dream den in the woods and what I should pack.

SUNDAY 12 SEPTEMBER

My step-dad, Nev, is filling the dishwasher and Mum is trying to make me think about homework. Homework is proof the world hates kids. She's laid all my books out on the kitchen table. I'm on the spinny chair. Nev's humming. The cat has her face in her dinner. The books. Mum. Nev. Cat. Books. Mum. Nev—

'Mo, come on. You've left it all until the last minute. We have biscuits, but you must do the homework to earn them.' Mum has her scruffy clothes on and her hair's up in a ponytail. She's put her hand on my chair to stop it spinning. 'Let's do maths first.'

'I hate maths.'

'It will have to be history then.'

'I love history,' says Nev, coming over. 'Whatcha studying? Henry VIII? 1066? The bubonic plague?' He makes a face and pretends his skin is bubbling with sores, then he grabs my shoulders. 'Heeeelp me!'

'Gerroff!' I laugh and push him. He pretends to

fall over and writhes about on the rug. The cat comes over to sniff his ear, then walks off with her bum in the air.

'Nev, even the cat thinks you're mad.' Mum laughs. 'It's Victorians actually.'

Nev jumps up and starts pretending he's a chimney sweep in *Oliver!* singing, 'Food, glorious food!'. Which is funny – in a cringe way – until Mum tells him to leave me alone to do some work.

I do the questions and Mum feeds me biscuits.

'So, are you enjoying your lessons then?'

I shake my head.

'Made any new friends?'

I shrug. 'I talked to one person.'

'You talked to someone?' Nev makes a shocked face.

'What? It's a big deal,' I say, spinning round again.

'Ooh, that's great love,' Mum says gently. 'Who is it?'

'She's called Carys.' I feel my mouth wanting to smile as I label the sources in my history book. 'I sit next to her in HWE and she drew me a shark.'

'She sounds nice love. You could invite her around for tea?' Mum suggests.

I wonder about whether I would do that. Whether we might become proper friends that go to each other's houses, like normal people. Whenever Ellie came to mine, it was Mum who arranged it. When

I think about it, it always made me feel sick, like she would find out about who I really am.

'Joined any sports clubs?' Nev interrupts my thoughts.

I shake my head again. 'They don't start until next week.'

'That'll be fun. You'll enjoy that. You should try netball,' Mum says.

'Football!' Nev sings from the kitchen.

'Maybe.'

'I spoke to Coach and she thinks after a couple of weeks back in routine practice, you should be able to compete again.'

I shut my book firmly, ignoring her comment. 'I'm all done.'

'What about packing your books back in your bag?' Mum says, as I shut the kitchen door and make my way upstairs.

I love my room. I properly LOVE it. It is *my* space and no one's allowed in if I don't want them. Mum painted me a mural on one wall last year. I still love it. It's a snowy mountainside with a snow leopard standing on the top of the mountain. She only used black and white. She is dead talented, my mum. I'm rubbish at art. Everything I try looks wonky or wrong. The only thing I've ever been any good at is gymnastics.

My medals dangle down from a hook on my shelf. I tug them off. I don't want them anymore, so I drop them into the bin. They 'tink' as they hit one another, the ribbons curling together in a tangled heap. That part of my life is over, whatever Mum thinks.

I hoped at secondary school I'd find a subject I was half good at, or at least that I *liked.* PE is okay, but so far all we've done is throw a ball about to each other to learn names, and then jogged around the sports hall because it was raining.

It's all such a drag.

I lie down on my bed and put my blanket across my face. No one knows this. No one will *ever* know this, but I still have a blanket. I sniff it. How weird is that?! Whenever I think about it, I feel very strange about it, but I've always had it. Ever since I was a baby. Mum says I never had a dummy, and I wasn't that bothered with teddy bears. I just loved my blanket. It helped me sleep, and it still does now. It's my secret.

I breathe in its smell. It smells of home. It feels so soft on my skin too and blocks out the light when I look through it. Since my diagnosis, Mum says she understands it more; she says it's a stim – what I do to calm myself down.

I'd love to take it to school but even I realise that would be utter social suicide.

Maybe I could put it on my face instead of looking at stooopid Ellie!

After a bit, I get out my phone. There are a load of new messages in the group chat from my form class. I don't know everyone's names yet. Ellie set up the group, of course. She's Miss Social Media, so by the end of day one in secondary school, she had everyone's names and numbers.

Some kid called Mylo has been spamming pictures of Yoda. Maya is getting cross with him. I'm a lurker. I don't post much. I asked a question on it about homework on the first day and Ellie told me not to be boring. I thought it was a school chat group? I wonder if Carys is on it. She hasn't posted anything at all.

I'd love to have a proper friend, someone who doesn't think I'm boring or embarrassing or *weird.* I hope tomorrow isn't toooo awful and I don't get another detention. Mum wanted to phone the school and complain about it, but I made her promise not to. I need to learn to deal with stuff on my own now. I'll give it one more week before I escape to the woods.

MONDAY 13 SEPTEMBER

I pull my school shirt over my head and it rubs against the rubbery blobs that have appeared, seemingly overnight, on my chest. More *ewwww*. I was flat-chested a few days ago. I press my chest with the palm of my hand, willing the blobs to retract. Go away!

Mum has big boobs. I really, really don't want boobs at all, let alone big ones. She moans about her achy back and the bras that dig in. They have wire round the bottom, like some medieval torture cage to trap the great blobs. If mine get that big I'll have surgery. Get them chopped off.

'Come on, Mo – we'll be late,' Nev calls up the stairs. I don't care about being late. It's Monday.

I hear him stomp up the stairs. He knocks on the door. 'Mo! It's half past.'

'I'm on the toilet!' I hiss. I am on the toilet. I'm sitting on the lid doomscrolling.

'I'll take your phone off you.'

Always with the threats…

When we line up for registration, I make sure I stand with Carys. Her hair looks totally different today. She has clips in her fringe to pull it away from her face and no earrings.

'I like your hair,' I say to try to get conversation going.

'I don't. I hate it,' she grumbles. 'My dad thinks my fringe is too long and says if I don't clip it back, he is going to cut it.'

'My dad doesn't care what my hair looks like,' I say, touching it over to check I actually remembered to brush it. I did.

'Lucky,' Carys replies as she roughly yanks the clips out. The last one gets stuck and dangles from her fringe like an awkward spider.

'Here.' I gently untangle the last one and pass it to her. She shakes her fringe forward into her eyes again and smiles. 'Thanks.'

After registration, it's maths. I'm feeling in a great mood after chatting to Carys. She is miles away from me though, by the window.

Miss Pool's voice drones from the front of the classroom, like a bee trapped under a glass: 'Blake Lennox?'

'Here.' The boy next to me raises his hand slightly.

'Maureen Prendergast?' She doesn't look at me, only at the monitor of her computer.

'It's Mo,' I say. Mum told me to tell all the teachers what name I prefer until they get the register changed.

'Pardon? Is Maureen here?'

'Yes, miss, but I prefer Mo.'

Miss Pool glares at me, unblinking. There is something about her that reminds me of a snake. She is so quiet, with eyes like hard marbles. I can imagine her swallowing students whole and soundlessly. 'Speak more loudly next time or you will be marked absent.'

I don't know if I'm expected to reply to that, so I start to get out my pens. The only good thing I have found about secondary school so far is that you get to bring your own pencil case. Mine is a fluffy dog. I've put a keyring I got from the theme park on the zip. You can spin the centre of the keyring and see what ride logo you get. I have to give it a quick spin. I get *Vengeance* three times in a row! What are the chances of that? Vengeance is the only ride I haven't been on yet. I think it must be a sign…

'MAUREEN! Did you hear what I just said?'

I look up. Miss Pool is staring down at me. Her fluffy grey hair and exploding eyebrows frame an expression that I DO know. Why are teachers always cross?

'No, miss.'

'I said, stop touching your pencil case and look at the board.'

I stop touching the pencil case and I look at the board.

'And stop tapping your feet.'

She says something I don't hear under her breath and a couple of the girls laugh on the front table and glance over at me.

'Okay, 7D, you have ten minutes to complete the task. There will be no talking.'

There are numbers scattered all over the board. There's something about minus numbers that I never understand. I mean if you have one cake how on earth can you have minus cakes? You have cake or you have no cake. Maths makes my brain shrivel up and die. The light from the window is causing a reflection, so I can't read all of the board. I look to see what the boy next to me is doing. He's written the title and date and he's drawing a table with columns and rows. He sees me looking and frowns, then puts his arm round his work.

Miss Pool isn't talking. She is sitting at her desk now plinky-plunking on her keyboard.

Everyone else is writing in their books. I can see Carys near the window, her head down over her work. Her fringe happily flopping over her face like a waterfall.

I glance at Miss Pool again. *Plinkyplunkyplinky plunky.* She said to stop touching my pencil case, but

I'm going to risk it. I reach out to unzip my dog and take out a biro and my ruler. *Phew.* She hasn't noticed. I write the date and title and remember to underline. There are so many rules and everyone here at Ysgol Offa seems so fussy about how stuff is done. I start to draw the table, but I've drawn a wonky line and I've used a pen so it's a mess and now I'm going to have to put a line through it and…

'Maureen. How come everyone else has completed the task and you are still drawing the table? Look at the state of this.'

Miss Pool's scaly hands pull my book off the desk and hold it up. Some other kids are sniggering.

'I wasn't sure what to do…'

'That's because you weren't listening at the start of the lesson.' She isn't shouting. She is speaking softly, but each word is like a flicker of her snake tongue. Mesmerising and dangerous. 'I will not have children who don't listen in my class.' She flaps my book about with the mess on the page. 'I will not have children who make no effort.' No one is laughing now. They are all watching, wondering when the snake is going to strike its prey.

'But you said don't touch my pencil case,' I say confused. 'And I couldn't see the board—'

Miss Pool's eyes lock on mine. Then she slithers

over and puts her fists on the desk in front of me. 'Are you backchatting me?' Her voice has gone even quieter, and I can hear the hiss in the words.

I can't keep eye contact, so my eyes fix on the slit of her mouth that is slightly open, ready for the kill.

'NO ONE BACKCHATS ME. GET OUT!' she suddenly shouts. There: strike. Eaten alive.

I leap out of my chair and rush for the door, leaving a desert of silence behind me.

'Oh, Mo.' Ellie bustles out of the class as the bell goes. 'You are gonna be in *so* much trouble. The rest of the class ripple around her like a river.

Maya pulls her ponytail tighter, checking the teacher isn't behind her, and links arms with Ellie. 'Yeah. My sister had Miss *Poo* in year eight. She is gonna *kill* you.'

They flutter away twittering to the yard where all the year sevens hang out. Carys is standing behind them. 'She is just the meanest teacher,' Carys says. 'Do you want me to wait for you?'

I'm too worried to speak but I nod gratefully, waiting for Miss Pool to come and shout at me.

Playtime – sorry, *breaktime* – is so boring in secondary school. There is nothing to do and no one plays games anymore. They just stand around chatting.

Some kick a football around the back, though that's mainly the older kids. There is no Capture the Flag or Last One Standing, which we played last term in my old school. Maybe Carys and I could go to the library together or—

The maths classroom door opens. 'What are you doing here?' Miss Pool snaps at Carys, propelling her away from me with her scaly finger.

'You, in.' Miss Pool nods to me to go back in the room. 'Sit.'

I sit.

'Complete the work you failed to do during the lesson.'

'But I can't see the board properly and I don't really understand it.'

She huffs and pulls out another chair nearer the board. 'Sit here then.'

I move places and look at the board. It is a bit clearer.

'So, I have to add that to that...?'

She snatches my book off me once more. 'You copy the example like this, and write your answer like this.' She jabs my book each time with a reptilian finger, then slaps it back in front of me.

Maths has now taken over from science as The World's Worst Subject.

I'm not really a crier, but I can feel misery stinging my eyes. I will not cry here. I will wait until I am home and safe. I take a pen out of my pencil case and slowly begin to copy down the work.

TUESDAY 14 SEPTEMBER

No maths today! History is interesting though and I think I have a new obsession coming on.

We're doing Victorians and the teacher – Mr Brock – is telling us about asylums and who ended up in them. He is talking about how some families put women in them because they fell in love with someone their family didn't like, or because they suffered *hysterics* – which basically covered any kind of depression or sadness or grief. He says people with disabilities would end up in them too, then he says, 'Like learning difficulties or *autism*.' I feel like a frog has lodged in my throat and I can't swallow. I have so many questions. I don't know if Mr Brock is nice or mean yet; I don't want to ask in case I get in trouble.

'There's a Victorian asylum down the road – Denham. It was still in use up until the 1990s when they finally closed it down,' Mr Brock says.

'Wasn't there a fire there, sir?' Sambhav asks.

'Yep. Some vandals got in and caused a lot of damage. It's really dangerous. Not a place to play, kids.'

'They filmed that ghost show there. I've seen some of it,' Mylo pipes up.

'I saw, yes. Ridiculous what some people watch these days…' Mr Brock says, stroking his beard absentmindedly.

When the bell goes everyone crowds out of the room. I'm hoping Carys might wait for me, but maybe she's decided I'm not worth hanging around for.

'I'm gonna go there one night and look for ghosts!' Sambhav grins.

'There's no such thing as ghosts,' I say, as I walk behind him.

'My nan's got one in her house.' Sambhav turns to me. 'It smashes things and one time I was staying overnight and it kept turning the light off and on. I've not stayed since.'

'She's probably just got dodgy wiring.'

'Yeah, but why do cups just break themselves?' he says animatedly.

Mylo nods.

'If she's next to a busy road, the vibrations from the cars can—' I stop talking. Sambhav has wandered off with his football mates, all still chattering on about ghosts and the asylum, and I am on my own.

I never get the fascination with ghosts. Scientifically they can't exist. People just like scaring themselves and it gets on my nerves. Asylums, though. I need to know more about Denham. What did they do to autistic people?

There's no sign of Carys anywhere, so I scurry to the library. There are no computers free, but Mrs Hughes shows me where the local history section is. There isn't anything on Denham asylum, but I find some pictures of it in *An Illustrated History of Brynffynnon.* The photos show a big building with serious-looking women dressed in black with white aprons on. There's one of a man in a wheelchair. Another of a ward with metal beds. I start to read about the 'ground-breaking' treatment for the mentally ill they'd used in the 1940s – electric shock treatment. It sounds horrendous.

'DRRRRRRRRINNNGG.'

The bell makes me jump every time. I can't imagine ever getting used to the awful sound of it. Mrs Hughes says I'm not allowed to get the book out as it is a reference one, but I know what I'll be doing when I get home.

By the end of my English lesson, I'm starving. It seems to take *sooo* long to get to lunch in secondary school. Still struggling with the zip on my bag, I'm the last one out of the classroom, yet again. But when I stumble out into the corridor, Carys is waiting for me.

A ridiculous grin parades across my face like a happy elephant – Carys waited for me!

'You still want to go to drama club?' she asks, twisting a leather braid around her wrist.

'Okay, though I don't know if I'll be able to do drama. I'm not that – you know.' I gesture with my hands, trying to articulate outgoing, confident – more like Ellie.

She nods as though she understands what I mean, and we start to walk up the corridor together. I'm hoping we can eat in drama club because my stomach feels like it's eating itself.

'Do you know where it is? I've got my map somewhere.' I still have no idea where I'm going. I feel about in my pocket when some bigger kids run past, pushing me into Carys. 'Sorry.'

'It takes some getting used to,' Carys agrees.

I find the map and we have a look at it together and work out which direction to go.

'So, which school did you come from?' I ask her as we walk with more purpose.

'I was home-schooled.' She lifts her head slightly and we make eye contact briefly. She's got brown eyes.

'Oh wow. Lucky.'

She shrugs. 'I went to St Mary's Primary but I didn't get on there so my mum took me out when I was eight. It was okay at home but a bit boring. I've come to secondary school to see if I like it.'

'I don't like it. I hate it. The teachers are mean.'

She shrugs again. 'Miss Pool is a *total cow.* Look, we're here.' She points to the door that says, Drama Studio.

I don't know what to expect but Carys has opened the door and she's holding it for me to follow her. The studio is bigger than all the other classrooms, and there are no tables and chairs. There are spotlights on the ceiling and there's a little stage at one end. There's a massive walk-in cupboard with its doors open wide and inside are HUNDREDs of costumes all hanging up, in every colour you can imagine. Some other kids are here already, sitting on the floor eating their lunches out of plastic boxes. Ellie is already here, hanging on Ms Latimer. Relief trickles through me as I realise there's no need to even try to talk to Ellie. I'm here with Carys.

Carys and I drop our bags where the others are. I rummage inside to find my packed lunch, pulling out the sandwiches. Always the same: cheese on brown bread – no butter. Mum's packed the usual other stuff: crisps, chocolate, apple – green ones only.

'God, Mo, no wonder you put weight on, eating all that lot!' Maya's arrived and is hovering above me frowning at my lunch.

My mouth pauses mid-chew as I process what she's just said to me.

'I just came to find Ellie. I didn't think you'd be here.' Maya looks around the room and then flits over to Ellie who is still glued to Ms Latimer.

'Who does she think she is?' Carys says, looking at me through her hair. 'It's none of her business what you eat for your lunch.'

'I know.' I finish chewing my mouthful miserably. 'They weren't always like this. I used to do gymnastics with them. I've left now.'

'I don't blame you. They're *awful*.' Carys nudges my arm with hers. 'Here swap.' She offers me part of her Twirl for part of my KitKat. 'Chocolate is loads better than gymnastics.'

The room is quite full now. I recognise faces from my class, but there are others from different classes too. Around the room are posters and photos of performances. I recognise some of them I've seen at the theatre: *Grease*, *The Wizard of Oz*.

Ms Latimer claps her hands to get us all to listen. 'Welcome to drama club!' She beams. 'I want you all to pick an object out of the prop basket.' She gestures to a giant plastic tub filled with hats and shoes, masks and scarves, as well as other things – a plastic apple, a set of old keys, toy guns and so on. A couple of the boys get there first and dive straight for the guns. I watch as people pick out a grandma handbag, a pair of specs, handcuffs, a wallet filled with fake notes. Carys gets hold of a white beard. I pick out a mohican wig.

'Okay now,' Ms Latimer calls. She waits until we're all quiet and then speaks again. 'There aren't many rules in the drama studio, but there are a couple.' She points to the door where a big poster says, Expectations. 'Drama is pretend, so no hitting or fighting, you must fake it, or you're banned! Respect each other and be kind, okay?' We all nod. 'Now I want you to think about what character you could be with the prop you've chosen. What are they like? How do they behave? Once you've worked that out, pair up with someone else. Imagine both your characters have met up in the park – what happens next? Off you go!'

I push my shoulder-length hair back and into the wig, tucking up the strands inside the plastic headpiece. The mohican sticks up on top and wobbles about. It is bright blue, red and white.

'You're a Neo-Nazi fascist.' Carys pokes my wobbly hair.

'Yeah,' I say, not sure what one is. I know Hitler was a Nazi, so I can guess it's not someone very kind.

'You look like Dumbledore,' I grin, as Carys hoops

the elastic about her ears and fluffs up the beard on her chest. Her fringe is scooped behind her ears too. She makes a gesture as though she has a wand in her hand and has just spelled me.

'No, Dumbledore! You're the greatest, you can't spell me,' I cry as I fall to the floor.

'But you don't deserve to live,' Carys says, her face full of anger, still holding her imaginary wand in the air.

'Just because I have a mohican doesn't make me a bad person!' I cry, getting up and holding my hands above my head like they do in shoot-out movies.

'You beat people up just for being different, for being Black or gay. You have no morals. I'm here to defend the good,' Carys says, stepping toward me menacingly.

'No, not me!' I back away from her shaking my head. 'I help old ladies across the road. I've got an allotment!' Still, she comes toward me. I am almost against the wall. 'I'm a vegetarian. I make my own goat's cheese!'

Carys bursts out laughing. 'You make your own goat's cheese?'

'Yes!' It's the first time I've seen her smile and it's catching. 'It's very tasty.' I start to grin too, and it feels great.

At the end of drama club Carys and I swap numbers. I don't speak in science; despite the fact the teacher is an imbecile and knows nothing about the Neogene period. It's lucky I'm more interested in history now.

By teatime Carys still hasn't messaged me and I don't know whether I should message her or not. I have a quick flick through the gymnastics group chat. They're all posting about the competition at the weekend. I hover my finger over **exit group** but can't bring myself to do it. I'll wait to see how the competition goes, then I'll leave.

Instead, I distract myself by doing some research on Victorian asylums. Bethlem was the oldest – that was in London. Some people called it Bedlam which is why people use the word 'bedlam' when something is crazy and noisy – because of how awful it was in there. Where you went depended on how rich you were because rich people put their families in nicer ones. Poor people went into charity ones where they were chained up and strapped to beds.

Nev is cooking chilli while I'm working on the laptop at the kitchen table. He sees me looking at pictures of the straitjackets – some had a cage for the face.

'What you doing, Mo?'

'Homework.'

'You don't do homework without a fight.' He grins.

'No, but this is interesting; it's about the asylums. Mr Brock said autistic people used to end up in asylums. People like me.'

'Not people like you, Mo – not even then. You are too high functioning—'

'Nev!' Mum comes to peer over my shoulder with a tea towel in her hand. 'You know I hate that phrase.'

Nev shrugs. 'But you know what I mean—'

'No! There is no such thing. Autistic people present in a whole load of different ways – "high" makes it sound like they are more superior to others. Who is *low* functioning?'

'I know, but Mo seems normal – not like, well, do you remember Bobby? He still can't speak.'

Mum is building up to danger point. I can always tell because her eyes go all pop-out and she threads her fingers in her hair like she's about to pull it out.

'Don't!' she yelps, her hair now on end like an electrocuted hedgehog. 'Stop with the "normal" and the – argh! – some autistics have other things going on like learning difficulties, but just because Mo can speak doesn't mean she's not struggling.'

'I know. I didn't mean that,' Nev says, irritation slipping into his voice.

'I am here you know.' I continue scrolling through the information on Bedlam. Mum is autistic too. Nev isn't. Mum thinks she has to educate Nev about it at every opportunity. I see her point. But it does get boring.

I stop at one of the photos on the screen. It is a black-and-white grainy photo of a man from the 1920s. He is in a straitjacket, curled up on a hard, dirty-looking floor. His face is caught mid-scream. It looks like the worst place in the world.

I realise they've gone quiet behind me. They're both looking at the image too.

Mum is silent for a minute. 'I had an uncle who was put in one of those places when he was a young man. He never came out.'

I turn to look at Mum. 'Was he autistic?'

'Maybe. People didn't talk about disabilities back then. There was a lot of shame in it for families – having someone who was different. Your taid didn't really talk about it until he was ill. Said he'd had an older brother who died in the asylum. I asked why he'd lived his life in the asylum and Grandad said all he remembered was that Albert used to have rages – maybe he was autistic.'

I look at the man on the screen. In another time, another place – that could've been me.

Ping.

My phone.

Ellie's had to shut the school chat down. Mylo started calling Leo gay. Leo got upset and told our teacher. Apparently, we are all too young to be using social media anyway.

It's an unknown number. An emoji of a frog. Just one.

I scrabble for my school bag and hunt for the bit of paper I wrote Carys' number on – could it be her? Typical me, I can't find it. I hunt in my pencil case and everywhere.

I'm not supposed to message strangers. I'm not stupid. I've had the talk at school, like, a hundred times already. I reckon this is Carys though. I message her back. I put two frogs and write: Carys?

There's no reply so I go back to looking at Denham on the laptop, when my phone pings again.

No. Onyx.

Who's Onyx? I message back.

I am your friend.

I'm getting the creeps now. I don't know whether to reply or not. I could tell Mum.

I don't know anyone called Onyx, I reply. There is a long pause where I stare at my phone screen with nothing happening.

Then, You may also know me as Dumbledore…

I'm completely puzzled for a moment until I remember: white wig, wizard hat – drama club!

Carys! You freaked me out.

I hate the name Carys. Call me Onyx.

KK. I put my phone down. Then type, Onyx at skool too?

She puts a skull emoji. I reply with a potato and we have emoji wars for about half an hour, then she messages, Dad home. Gotta go.

I think about school as I'm drifting off to sleep and instead of the usual hedgehog of misery lodged in my stomach, there's a grin back on my face. Carys actually seems to like me!

FRIDAY 17 SEPTEMBER

Carys, or Onyx, wasn't in yesterday. She didn't reply to my message last night and she's not in today either. Having a proper friend – it was too good to be true.

At breaktime I go to the canteen following the rest of my class. Maya is in front of me when I join the queue.

I'm minding my own business, counting the people in front of me, when Maya turns round.

'Mo, you need to stop following us around.'

I stare at her blankly. 'I'm not—'

One of the wannabes joins in. 'Where's your little freak friend?'

Another giggles. 'Oh yeah, the emo.'

It takes me a moment to compute that they are talking about Carys. I'm about to tell them that she's off today, but stop myself. This is not a kind conversation. They don't really want to know, do they? *Freak. Emo.* The words take a moment to process, to connect.

'I know we hung out in primary, Mo,' Ellie says. I can see her gum as she chews. 'But that was coz of gymnastics.'

'And your mum.' Maya laughs.

'Oh yeah, my mum says she was *relentless*.'

They're laughing again. Laughing mouths, chewing gum flickering. I just want to get to the till and pay for my drink.

'*Please let Ellie come for a sleepover*,' she mimics. '*My daughter's got no friends*.'

I don't want to listen to them. I think about dumping the drink, but I've forgotten my bottle and I'm already dying of thirst.

'Yeah, you don't really fit with us anymore, y'know?' Maya says. 'You need to stay away from us.'

I want to put my hands over my ears. I can feel the bite of tears. 'I'm just getting a drink!' I say.

Everyone in the queue stops talking and stares at me.

'No need to shout about it,' a wannabe says, and the others start giggling. We've reached the till. They turn their backs on me and flutter away. I stand in the canteen, the bottle in my hand, while the rest of the kids pour around me like water.

At lunchtime I make it to drama club on my own without getting too lost.

'Welcome everyone!' Ms Latimer grins. 'So, today we are going to develop your character ideas from Tuesday and make a little sketch. Aim to have something change in your scene – it doesn't have to be a big change. It could be two friends falling out. Or one of your characters could be hungry and need a meal. We will watch a few before the bell goes.'

Everyone dives for the props in the prop basket. I wait my turn and collect my wig. I look about. I can't develop my scene and don't have anyone to work with. I wonder if I should leave and go to the library instead, but Ms Latimer comes over to me.

'No Carys today? No worries.' Ms Latimer beams. 'Just make a three.'

Ellie and Maya are working together, but I steer away from them. I catch the word 'emo' again. Ellie shakes her hair over her face in an imitation of Carys.

I step more decisively over to Soraya and Chantelle who were in my primary. 'We're doing a wedding scene,' Chantelle says.

'You can be the wedding photographer,' Soraya suggests.

Boring. I don't say it but I think it, and maybe they can mind read because they turn their backs on me too.

I wander about with my wig on watching what the others are doing. I join Harry's group for a few moments but he and Sambhav just keep shooting me, saying I'm the robber.

‘Don’t want to join a group, Mo?’ Ms Latimer says to me.

I shrug.

‘Why don’t you look in the cupboard and see who you want to be? Pick a costume. Make sure you put things back on their hangers though, okay?’ She pats me on the shoulder, propelling me toward the costume cupboard.

The costume cupboard is my new favourite place. Some of the outfits smell a bit weird, but all the colours, the fabrics! I try on a rabbit outfit – sooo soft (*Alice in Wonderland* – Ms Latimer says). Then there’s a chimney sweep outfit – kind of rough (*Oliver!*), and an insect – plasticky in places (*The Insect Play*?).

The insect is my favourite. I’ve never thought about what it would be like to be a grasshopper. It goes over my head and pulls down to my knees, like a skirt. Three bendy plastic legs dangle either side of my thorax, and a hood with bulbous black eyes lifts over my hair.

‘Good choice.’ Ms Latimer grins at me. ‘Come out and watch the sketches – I need your opinion.’

I leave the costume cupboard and go sit on a stool with my six legs dangling either side.

‘So, you ever done drama before?’ Ms Latimer asks me as the first pair get ready to show.

'No, but I used to do gymnastics and do competitions.'

'Oh, Ellie was telling me all about gymnastics,' Ms Latimer says, settling into a stool next to me. There is something in the way she speaks the words that makes me want to listen. 'Apparently she's the best gymnast in Brynffynnon.' She raises her eyebrows slightly in a way that makes me smile.

We watch all the sketches one by one. Ellie and Maya's performance is dull, though Ms Latimer praises them for being 'full of confidence'. Harry and Sambhav's is just daft, though it does make me laugh. Ms Latimer makes me vote on my favourite and I give them my vote as they're the funniest – though I don't think it's on purpose.

'On Tuesday we're going to do a little acting from a script. There will be a chance for everyone to speak.' Her eyes glance over to me. 'Okay, everyone. Props back in the basket.'

I go back to the cupboard and pull the insect suit over my head, but it gets stuck. The bell rings for afternoon lessons. I tug some more. I'm going to be late.

'Want any help?' says a voice.

'Yes please,' I say into one of the grasshopper's armpits.

The next thing, the suit is lifted off my head and I'm free. A tall person is in the doorway holding the suit, a smile tugging at the corner of their mouth. I think it's a girl, but it is hard to say. They have short, bleached hair and four or five earrings. They're wearing a white T-shirt with a tongue sticking out on it, and tracksuit bottoms.

'You okay?' they say.

'Yeah. Thanks.' I'm staring. 'Why're you not in uniform?' Falls out of my mouth before I have chance to pause.

They laugh. 'I'm doing my exams this year. We're allowed to change into something else when we are doing drama. You gonna get to class?'

'Oh yeah. Thanks.'

'No problem, little bug.'

I rush past them, waving at Ms Latimer and banging my bag against the door handle on my way out.

Dad picks me up from school in his manky van. It's so good to see him and he gives me the biggest hug. Stink's in the car grinning from his car seat. He clacks his rattle in my direction.

'One more sleep!' Dad says excitedly.

It takes me a moment to remember the trip to Blue Zoo at the weekend. I know enough about people that he is going to be upset if I tell him my interest in piranhas is on the wane. This is what happens with my special interests. They are all intense and then, poof! They just disappear and I'm left wondering what all the fuss was about. I mean, I do still like piranhas, but it isn't what is on my mind right now.

I manage a smile back at Dad, but then proceed to fill him in on the Victorian health system as he navigates the traffic out of School Lane and onto the main road.

'Do you know where Denham is, Dad?' I ask, as I unwrap a sherbet lemon and stuff the wrapper in the door compartment.

'Where's that?'

'Denham asylum. Mr Brock says it's near here.'

'Oh, right, the old hospital. It's in town. We drive past it in a couple of minutes. On your side. Behind the big supermarket. You'll have seen it before.'

I watch out of the window, waiting to see. We get stuck at a red light again and then the shop logo appears.

'Go slow!'

'I can't stop completely.'

The flat white roof of the supermarket is in the way, but I can see another roof behind, very different from the gleaming metal one. This roof is taller and pointy. It has sharp gables with gaps in the slates where some have slipped. Dad's right, I have seen it loads of times, but never knew what it was – just an old, ruined building. But now I know it is Denham asylum that hunches on the other side of the supermarket like a spiky giant.

'You see it?'

'Yeah, a bit. Can we stop?'

'Aw, not today, MoMo. Diane's got Zumba.' We are driving away now, toward the other side of town where Dad's house is. 'Anyway, I'm pretty sure it burnt down – a couple of years ago, y'know. What's left has been sold. They're planning on bulldozing the lot, I think, turning it into flats.'

'Can I go see it tomorrow?'

'Why the obsession with the asylum then, MoMo?'

I nibble at my lip while I try to think of an answer. My answer is bubbly like fizzy water and impossible for me to form into words. Screaming man. A disappeared great uncle. Autism. Interesting and weird and scary. The nurses with the straitjackets. It could've been me. I bet Miss Pool would have put me in there straightaway if she could, and Ellie, blaming me for her falling over after science.

But that all sounds … weird – so I shrug instead.

'It's private property, Mo. You can't visit,' Dad says, as we turn into our road.

As soon as we get home we have tea, as Diane's going out. Then while Dad's bathing Stink – no, I don't want to help – I go online to search for Denham. The main search is all about the ghost show they filmed there. There are loads of pictures of what it looks like now – rooms covered in scrawling graffiti and broken windows. There are pictures after the fire – blackened beams and roofs caved in. There are pictures of rooms still with old floral wallpaper on the wall, a single wheelchair. A dark corridor.

I have to visit and go inside.

SATURDAY 18 SEPTEMBER

The car park at Blue Zoo is pretty chocka already. I hate busy places normally, but there is something about the aquarium: even when it's full, it feels sort of calm and chilled out. All the fish that gawp back at me look like they're having silent conversations and I don't have to worry about the words.

It takes ages to get out of the car and into the reception. Stink has so much stuff! Buggy, bag with nappies and all that. Bag with food in. It was easier when he was just on milk, but now he needs bibs and pots and bowls. Then Dad's left his phone in the car, but Diane wants him to take photos so we have to go back.

I'm kicking the dead leaves and little stones against the kerb. The stones bounce off and I look to see how far I can get them to bounce. One hits the window of Blue Zoo with a nice 'toc' sound. I do it again with a bigger one.

'Oi you!' a voice calls from behind me. I turn and see a tall man in a business suit just clambering out of his car. He is pointing a finger at me. 'Stop that thuggish behaviour. You will break the glass!'

I feel shame nettle my skin, despite knowing that the massive window would never be broken by the tiny stone I'd kicked. I wonder whether I should explain but he's walked off.

'Why don't you look round the shop?' Diane suggests.

I shrug and head off. Stink yells 'MahMah?' after me, but I don't look back. I love shopping!

Last time I was here was over a year ago. It looks different. Smaller. The toys don't interest me anymore. I spot the slime pots I was really into last time I was here and the big plastic sharks. I bet Stink would enjoy chewing on those. I look at the jewellery stands. There's way too much pink. Silver necklaces with BFF on them. I like the shark-tooth necklaces and the bracelets though.

'Mo? No way!'

I turn round. There is the gigantically tall man who just yelled at me and a tidy woman with short brown hair and glasses, and between them is Onyx. Her hair is brushed to the side and there are those clips again holding it back. She's wearing leggings and a blue hoodie with 'Superstar' written across it.

'Hey.' I smile nervously.

'Do you know *this* person, Carys?' the man says in disgust.

Carys is about to speak when, at that moment, Dad practically falls through the door. He's got the coats over his arm and the food bag over the other. Diane follows with Stink in the pram, who looks like he's turned into a noisy strawberry – all red and round and squawking.

'Mo!' Dad seems to have momentarily lost his smile. 'Stink's hungry and we forgot the snacks.'

'You forgot the snacks,' Diane says quietly.

'Well, anyway, we'll need to feed him before we go round the zoo. Oh, hi.' He finally notices Onyx's family watching my family as though they are one of the exhibits.

'This is O—' I start to say, but Onyx's eyes open wide and she shakes her head at me. '…Carys. She's a fr… someone from school.'

'Hello,' says Dad, over Stink's shrieks. 'You enjoying Ysgol Offa?' He directs this to Onyx.

'It's okay. This is Mo, Mum,' Onyx says to the tidy woman, not including her dad in the conversation.

'Pleased to meet you, Mo. It's wonderful that Carys has made a friend. Being home-schooled she was rather nervous about starting, but was adamant she wanted to give it a go.'

Onyx looks embarrassed.

'Oh, it's a big change for them, isn't it?' Dad

agrees. His eyes flicker over to Diane and Stink – who sounds as though he is trying to crack glass with his ear-splitting shrieks.

'Oh dear – little one's hungry?' Carys' mum asks.

'Yes, we need to go and give him a top up, I think.' Dad smiles.

'Do we have to go to the cafe first?' I complain. 'We've only just arrived.'

'We need to sort Ewan out, Mo,' Diane says firmly.

'I could go look on my own?' I ask.

'Well—'

Onyx's mum catches the glances Onyx and I are giving each other and asks, 'Why doesn't Mo tag along with us? We can see you in there if you like? That's okay, isn't it, George?'

'I was looking forward to a family day.' Onyx's dad crosses his arms and frowns. Onyx looks at him silently and there is an awkward pause that is lost on my dad who is too busy rooting through the baby bag.

'Just for a few minutes, George,' Onyx's mum responds gently.

'Can we trust this girl to behave properly? I'm not convinced she knows how – kicking rocks against windows,' Onyx's dad declares, tipping back slightly on his heels.

'Mo will behave perfectly, won't you, Mo?' Diane

says, placing her hand on my shoulder as I open my mouth to defend myself.

'Well, remember we have to leave at 2 p.m.' Onyx's dad huffs and walks toward the entrance without speaking again.

'Yes!' Onyx grins and jumps.

I run over to her. 'I'll see you later!' I call to Dad and Diane.

'Okay, well, be good, and thank you!' Dad says, as Onyx and I rush through the entrance into the first exhibit.

'Were you poorly?'

Onyx looks at me confused.

'You weren't in school yesterday,' I remind her.

'Oh, yes. Sort of,' she says.

'I messaged you, but you didn't answer.'

Instead of answering me, she changes the subject. 'Have you been here before?' Onyx asks me. As we both stare at the carp, their gold diamond skin flashing in the lights from the tank.

'Yeah, loads. Piranhas have been one of my things for ages. You?' I ask trying to remember how conversation is supposed to work.

It feels great to be with Onyx, but embarrassing too. It is all out of place. I am *home* me, not *school* me.

'I came a few times with Mum when she was

schooling me. I know all about the life cycle of a fish.' She looks skywards. 'My faves are the piranhas, too.'

'They always feed them at 12!' I say excitedly and we jog past the exhibits to the giant tank where the sharp-toothed creatures are darting, waiting for meat. There is already a crowd building, but Onyx wriggles in and pulls me with her so we can watch. Her parents are somewhere near the back.

'So, you're not Onyx in front of the parents then?' I ask, as we stare into the tank looking at the steady pace of the fish as they flicker back and forth.

'Nah. I don't like my name. I want to change it, but Dad won't let me.' Onyx glowers behind her, checking her parents are out of earshot.

'I don't like *Maureen* either. It's so old – my nanna's name. I prefer Mo.'

'Mo's cute.'

'So, I call you Onyx but not in front of parents or teachers? I'm autistic, so I can't promise I'll not fail at this.' I prattle, hardly realising I've said what I have until it is out there, hanging about in the air like a surprised turtle.

'Actually, are you?' Onyx blinks at me.

'Am I what?'

'Autistic?'

'Oh that, yes.'

Should I have told her? I sometimes overshare without realising until it's too late.

But Onyx just shrugs. 'Cool.' She pauses for a moment. 'You can use Onyx in school. I don't care what other people think.'

The aquarium keeper comes with the bucket full of bloody entrails and starts to load them into the tank through a hatch. I wish I didn't care what other people think, but I'm always doing things wrong. I have a feeling Onyx's dad hates me already! I watch the pieces of flesh plop into the water and blood billow out in inky patterns. The fish begin to move faster and faster.

'So why did you get home-schooled?' I ask.

'I did go to a primary school for a while but I didn't fit in well. There was some mean stuff and Mum said I could take a break. Dad wasn't keen, though. He never is.'

I watch the frenzy of teeth as the placid fish turn into silver gnashing darts. I wonder about the words I heard her called at school: *emo* and *freak*. I wonder if she's heard them too.

'It's weird being able to see your face,' I say, nodding to the clip.

'Oh God, this?' She pulls the clip out and ruffles her hair forward. 'My dad has weird ideas about how girls should look. He drives me mad. A lot of the time he works away and Mum's okay, but Dad…' She throws the clip on the floor and crushes it under her foot. 'I wish I could feed him to the piranhas.'

She doesn't speak for ages, just stands there staring as the fish finish demolishing the food. Then a thought pops in my head.

'Hey, do you want to go to Denham with me?' As soon I've said it, I realise that this is probably not how normal people communicate, that there should be lots of really boring small talk first, but I really want to go and, if Onyx doesn't care about what people think, maybe she will be able to help me get there.

Onyx laughs and turns her attention away from the piranhas. 'Where?'

'Denham. It's an old Victorian asylum. You know Mr Brock has been going on about it in history. Denham's in town…' and I proceed to tell Onyx all about the asylum. 'There're pictures online. I've just got to see it for myself. Dad won't let me go, he says it's private property, but I reckon we could get in.'

'I thought I was weird but you're something else, Mo.' Onyx grins at me as we start to wander toward the next exhibit. 'Sure, why not? My dad's away next week and Mum is much more easy going. Sounds interesting. Anything my dad would hate is good with me.' She flickers her gaze in her parents' direction.

'Oh, they won't let us go. It's got to be a secret.'

'Sure.'

'So, where do you live? My dad lives not too far away from Denham – we could walk.'

'I'm up by the park. We could go after school? I'll tell my mum I'm going to homework club.'

'Okay. I'm at my dad's on Wednesday.'

'Let's do it.'

TUESDAY 21 SEPTEMBER

Whenever Onyx and I are together, we talk about going to explore the asylum. Even though she doesn't text me much at home, when we are in school she seems to really like me; she tucks her arm tight through mine and we walk around but without going anywhere in particular. It feels so *safe*. This is what the others do, the normal ones – hang about at breaktime. I can feel a kind of gurgling warm feeling scuttering up from my stomach, like I've just eaten pancakes. I've got someone to hang around with, and it's someone who seems to like me just the way I am.

It's breaktime and we are waiting in the English corridor for the bell to go, sneaking peeks at our phones when there are no teachers about.

'I found this.' Onyx shows me a blog on her phone called Paranormal UK. I look over her shoulder scanning the text. Someone has written that the number of ghostly sightings at Denham are the most for any building in the UK. Onyx seems almost as obsessed as me now, but I'm not sure we have the same reasons for being interested.

I'm about to explain how ghosts can't be real when Ellie, Maya and the wannabes rush past us giggling and I hear one of them say, 'Emo'. Just loud enough for us to hear.

Onyx doesn't say anything, but looks at me and pretends to flick her hair over her shoulder in a perfect imitation of Maya and we both start giggling.

English is boring, but it isn't long until lunchtime and today is drama club. We dump our bags in the usual place. I have a bit of my sandwich.

Ellie and her friends are already here trying on hats from a box. 'I know she didn't do as well as us, but I thought Nina did well getting bronze.'

'You did amazingly, Ellie,' Maya chirps. 'Another gold.'

'Thanks!' Ellie grins.

They aren't looking at me but I feel like they are talking to me. I try not to feel too glad that Nina didn't do that well, even though I don't want to go to gymnastics anymore.

'Why do they always try to wind you up?' Onyx whispers to me.

I look up from my cheese sandwich. 'Do they?'

'Yes!' Onyx looks surprised. 'Talking really loudly about how amazing they are at gym just when you arrive. They are so mean! It's a good job you've got me now.' She hooks her arm through mine, turning our backs to them.

'Besties,' she grins at me. I've never had a *best* friend before. I feel like a happy balloon.

Just then, Ms Latimer clears her throat and everyone goes quiet.

'Okay, we are all going to have a go at reading from a script today. Lara and Ifan are helping me out.' Ms Latimer gestures to the older students. One is a tall boy with the start of a moustache. The other is the one who rescued me from the insect costume – Lara.

'Hey, little bug,' Lara says as she hands me a script.

I smile, happy she's remembered me.

'And little bug's mate?' She hands a script to Onyx who nods at her.

Onyx stares at Lara, taking the book from her hand. As Lara continues handing them out, Onyx whispers, 'Oh my God, she is amazing.'

I shrug, not sure what she means, noticing her face has gone all red. Instead, I read the title on the front, *One Act Plays for Secondary Schools*. Catchy.

'Turn to page 46 – *Shipwreck*,' Ms Latimer says.

There is a list of characters and people are starting to call out all at once.

'Miss, can I be Sheila?'

'Can I be Captain?'

'Shhhh! Hands down. I'm going to tell you who you are.' Ms Latimer goes through the list choosing parts. 'Mo, I want you to be Ship's Cat.'

I skip through to see what Ship's Cat gets to say. 'Miaow' probably. Onyx gets the chorus with Soraya and another kid whose name I don't know.

We all stand in a circle and start to read. It is a daft story about a drunk Captain in a storm. Sambhav plays the Captain. He reads quite well. Ellie is Sheila and is being over-dramatic, as usual. Everyone laughs at first, but it starts to grate.

'It's wonderful to add expression to our voices,' Ms Latimer says, smiling. 'But we do need to be able to hear the words and follow what's going on.'

Luckily, Sheila is only in the first two pages. Ellie keeps whispering and flicking the pages loudly, looking to see where she comes in again. Ifan goes to stand next to her and puts his finger to his lips, signalling that Ellie needs to stop being a pain in the bum.

'Hey Captain, Captain dear, come here,' I say. The script says 'gestures' so I automatically use the hand not holding the script to beckon the Captain over.

'I can help you find the treasure,
if you will give me the pleasure,
of the fish on that there table.
And hurry, whilst you are able.'

I say the last line as though I'm doing a loud whisper to the audience.

I don't know why or how I feel so good doing this, but I do. I think being a bestie to someone makes you feel like you can do anything.

Ms Latimer gives me a beaming smile.

It says in the directions that Sambhav's character *acts drunk and knocks a plate on the floor, then falls into a heap and starts snoring*. But he doesn't do any of the actions, even though that is the most fun part.

Then it's my turn again.

'That will do just fine.
Mmm, I've tasted nicer,
but this can be the appetiser.
I think I might just help myself to the beef.
I don't think this man's in any state to care where
I sink my teeth!'

I pretend I'm jumping up on the table and tucking into the Captain's feast.

The chorus comes in then and the next scene.

'Bravo. Bravo.' Ms Latimer claps and so do the helpers. 'Well done, everyone. Great listening, and great reading too. The bell's going to go in a minute so we will leave it there for today.'

'Thanks,' Lara says to Onyx, taking the script from her. Onyx doesn't speak. She just stands there, still red in the face.

'Hey bug, you are great at acting,' Lara says, as she takes the script back from me.

'Am I? Thanks,' I say, smiling.

'Yeah. You know just where to add emphasis and don't rush your lines.'

'You're okay,' Maya cuts in, handing her script to Lara. 'I think you could put a bit more expression in, though.'

'Oh yeah?' Lara keeps her gaze on me. 'I think you got it just right. And the nose twitching was cute.'

Maya hangs around, but Lara walks off ignoring her.

I'm just trying to find my black bag, among the pile of all the other black bags, when Ms Latimer says my name.

'Mo, you read so well! Have you done acting before?'

'Only messing about at home, with my mum. Not in front of people.'

'Well, we're going to be looking for people to take part in the December show. The school does a different one every year. It isn't like a Christmas nativity. Last year we did *Grease*, and the year before it was *Little Shop of Horrors*. It would be great if you auditioned.'

'Oh right. I don't… I'm not sure I…'

'I know it can be a nerve-wracking thought, but I think you have got a real talent there. If you're used to audiences with your gymnastics – it isn't much different.' She pauses and keeps her gaze on me. I don't know what to say. My eyes are roving the bag pile still.

'Well, at least think it over. It will be a couple of weeks until we start to advertise. We're still arguing over which show to do!'

'Okay. Thanks.'

'See you next time.' She smiles at me.

I still can't find my bag, but then I see Onyx at the doorway holding it. She pulls me out of the door and drags me along the corridor. 'Oh, she is the most amazing person I've ever seen!'

'Who? Ms Latimer?'

'No! Lara!' Onyx holds her hands to her heart as we walk up the corridor to our next lesson.

WEDNESDAY 22 SEPTEMBER

The supermarket car park has embankments with bushes on the slope. Behind the bushes is a tall fence with concrete posts and barbed wire at the top. Behind all that, the asylum rises, dark and ominous.

'We'll never get over that,' I say, staring up at the fence.

'Never say never.' Onyx grins at me. 'Come on, there must be a way.'

She starts to walk the length of the car park. It ends at a busy dual carriageway that takes the traffic out of Brynffynnon towards the motorway. We can see the asylum roof – sharp and dark against the skyline. The fence rises, unbroken, beside the lanes of cars.

'Not that way then,' I say.

'Think about it, though, there must've been a way for people to get into the building, a gate or something. We need to get to it from the other side. Come on!' Onyx looks excited. She grins and grabs the arm of my coat, pulling me along with her.

We've come straight from school and still have

our school bags on our backs. They bump as we run, like badly-fitting turtle shells.

There is a pedestrian entrance to the supermarket that takes us along a walkway and joins a shopping street. I don't come here much, but I've been once or twice to the office-supplies store. A few people are walking with shopping bags in their hands, though a lot of the shops have 'For Sale' signs up now, and it is fairly quiet.

A little lane that leads behind the shops opens up on the right. It is cobblestone and mud, and it leads to the backs of the buildings where big bins are pushed up against dreary blank walls. On the other side of the lane, grass and shrubs lead to the same fencing that surrounds the old asylum. Here though the fencing has tag names sprayed on it: *Gizmo* in bold blue and gold, *Fierce* in yellow and black, as well as a whole load of graffiti I can't read.

'Promising!' Onyx jumps a little at she trots up the road backwards and gives me the thumbs-up.

'Look!' I point up ahead where a 'Private Property' sign has been bolted to the fence. Underneath it, someone has forced a way through the wooden panelling and tracks in the grass show people have got in through it. I chase to overtake Onyx, getting there at the same time.

‘Go on. This is your thing,’ Onyx says, stepping back slightly to let me go first.

I hesitate, staring at the sign, suddenly worried. I’m desperate to go in, to look for myself, but…

‘Do you think we should? If it’s private?’

‘No one will mind.’ Onyx grins at me. ‘They only put signs up like this so that no one sues them – if there’s an accident or something.’

‘Oh.’

I kneel and peek through the gap. Denham’s walls are tall and forbidding, dark with damp. The roof has caved in. Blackened struts stick out at weird angles, like mouldy bones.

A gentle nudge in the small of my back propels me forward, under the broken fence and into Denham’s grounds.

‘Cool,’ Onyx whispers beside me, her hands on her hips as she gazes over the site too.

Grass grows almost as tall as me, run through with brambles, browning bracken and nettles. There are red and white signs stating, ‘Trespassers Will Be Prosecuted’ and ‘Danger Do Not Enter’.

But it is the shadows that stop me.

That and the silence.

There is no sun this afternoon, but the great hulk of Denham casts a shadow over us. The traffic noise from town seems to have paused at the fence too, unwilling to enter this place.

Is it dangerous in there? And who made those tracks in the grass? I glance at Onyx. She pushes her hair away from her eyes and smiles at me, her eyebrows raised. 'What do you think?'

'Do you think it's dangerous?'

'Let's go a bit closer.' She steps toward the building, almost crouching as she moves. I keep reminding myself to breathe, then I follow Onyx.

We step around to the front of the building. It is barely recognisable from the photos online. There is so much fallen debris, blackened by the fire. Slates, guttering, bricks and wood clutter the walls like an ugly skirt. I can still see the steps leading to what was once the front door. The ground floor windows and the door are shuttered with metal guards. Upstairs the blank spaces gape, full of black shadows.

'Who else d'you think comes here?' Onyx asks me, her hand resting lightly on my arm.

'Dog walkers?' I look around at the big space where a garden used to be. *Murderers. Criminals*, my mind thinks. 'Kids?'

'Maybe,' she murmurs, head on one side.

We could go back. We could creep through the gap in the fence and go to the shop, buy sweets and go home. I could forget about Denham – its strange empty rooms, the cages. The autistic people that were held here all their lives. I could, but I don't. There is something about this place that is drawing me in. I have to explore it for myself and, now I've got Onyx with me, I feel that we can do anything we want.

'There must be a way in. Come on.' Onyx has hold of my jacket tugging me with her.

My heart bickers in my chest as we pelt across the open space. A seagull makes its way lazily across the sky, making me flinch. We reach the wall.

'Nailed shut,' Onyx says, as she pulls at the metal window grills.

There is graffiti here too, though less colourful, just white and black signatures across the brick and metal.

Each window is barred to us.

We move around to the back of the building, clambering over the fallen debris as we do so. 'SNAP!' A slate cracks under my weight, sparking a flicker of panic on Onyx's face.

Bigger trees grow here. A horse chestnut bends its weight, full of glistening brown conkers. Crows fling themselves up and away as we rustle our way round. I catch a splinter from a broken beam as I clamber over.

Then we find it.

A loose grill. It has been prised open at the bottom corner and opens like the leaf of a book, ready for us to enter.

'Really want to do this?' Onyx asks me, her face a patchwork of fear and excitement.

And though my mind is saying, NO! NO! NO! my head nods a silent, Yes!

Dumping my bag, I squeeze the top half of my body through. It looks as though this was some kind of kitchen or utility room. The walls are dirty-white and a work bench lines the wall, its legs buckled and broken. The sill I am balanced on is beside a metal sink with a rusted hole where a tap once was.

'Okay?' Onyx's voice asks.

'Yep. One minute,' I say, and pull myself onto the sink, that luckily holds my weight. Onyx pushes our bags through to me and then clambers in after them.

The smell is what hits me first. Musty and heavy, rotten and sour. It is quiet. Still. The work bench has cupboards above it. We open them carefully. 'There're cups still here!' Onyx says picking up a mint-green teacup and showing me.

'Plates too.' I hold one up to show her, its surface stippled with black and brown bits of something rank.

The metal grills over the windows only allow a speckling of light, but I can see two doors leading off the room. One is half open, leading to a corridor beyond. Silence seems to crawl through the gap towards us.

The other door is shut.

I make for the open door. Grit and dirt and the odd broken piece of crockery clutters the lino as we creep across it.

I take my phone out and turn on the torch, flicking the light into the dark. The corridor has doors leading off it, ending in some stairs. Onyx is listening again. The crows have come back outside, but other than that I hear nothing.

The doors lead to walk-in cupboards, empty apart from dust and decay, and a small bathroom. The toilet has an old chain handle fastened to a black cistern high up on the wall. Onyx lifts the toilet seat.

'Bleurgh!' she cries dropping the lid. The sound echoes against the walls.

'Don't look. There is crap in there.' She holds her nose and walks back out. 'Come on, let's go up the stairs.'

Onyx begins to clamber. The stairs have the same lino on them, curling at the edges. I tread carefully, thinking about rotten wood as I step one at a time.

'Woah.'

We are in the grand entrance hall. Grand once, perhaps. Bits of the collapsed ceiling cover the floor.

A lampshade lies on its back like a giant woodlouse. There is part of a reception desk, smooth rich wood still visible in places. In the centre of the hall, a great staircase leads upwards, still carpeted, and at the top a big stained-glass window lets in the light. I take some photos. It looks stunning and strange.

Wide corridors lead off in all directions, though one is almost completely blocked by chunks of roof. I look up and realise that I can see the sky blinking back at me.

'Where now?' Onyx asks.

'Up.'

The stair carpet is mouldy and threaded with moss. Onyx runs up the stairs and stands looking down at me.

'Welcome!' she shouts, flinging her arms above her head dramatically.

The clap and frantic rush of wings fills the roof space, as pigeons fly from hidden perches, above us.

I step back, tripping over my own feet.

'Crap!' Onyx says laughing. 'Mo – you okay?'

'I thought we were going to die,' I say, not exaggerating. My heart tries to stop yoyoing and settle back where it belongs. The birds do the same, roosting high up on the skeletal remains of the roof. 'Let me take your pic.'

Onyx poses at the top of the stairs then I run up to her. She takes my hand and we continue.

Bedroom after bedroom, with tiny metal beds, broken basins and peeling wallpaper.

'No cages,' Onyx says.

'No wards.'

'More like an old people's home,' Onyx says with disappointment, as we trudge back along yet another corridor.

'It stinks,' I say, sniffing in the smell of mouldy leaves and rotten carpets.

Suddenly, the sound of a duck quacking fills the air.

'Oh crap,' I fumble for my phone. 'It's my dad! It's nearly six! What do I say?'

'Say you're at mine but just leaving and you'll be home in twenty minutes,' Onyx says.

'Hi, Dad?... Yeah. I'm at Onyx... Carys' house... Oh... Near the park... No, I'll walk. I won't be long. Okay. Sorry I didn't know. Bye.' I put the phone off and turn to Onyx. 'He's cross I didn't come back for tea. He's taking my step-mum to her class. I've got to go.'

We follow our tracks back through the old building. Even the birds have gone quiet now. There's just the sound of our footsteps as we make our way down to the old kitchen.

'Basement!' Onyx grabs me and jumps up and down.

'Huh?'

'They're not going to keep the really mad ones on show, are they? They'll have kept them somewhere out of sight,' Onyx says excitedly.

'They weren't mad! They were just different. Because they didn't fit in, they were kept… ah, like in an attic or basement! I see what you mean.' I grin.

'We tried all these doors,' Onyx says as we walk back toward the kitchen. 'There must be another way. Another staircase to part of the basement.' Onyx passes me my bag out through the window. 'Well, you know what that means don't you? We're just going to have to come back.'

THURSDAY 23 SEPTEMBER

'You enjoyed yourself then, yesterday with Carys?' Dad asks.

He's off work today and is sitting at the breakfast table with me. Stink is on his knees stuffing a plastic train in his mouth.

'Yeah. Her parents call her Carys, but she prefers Onyx.'

'Oh right, okay. And where does she live? Yes, train!' Dad makes a goo-goo face at Stink.

'Ah!' Stink takes the train out of his mouth and grins at Dad.

'Up by the park,' I say, hoovering up my floating Wheetie Os.

'Yeah, you said that yesterday. The park's a big place, though, the duck-pond side or the skate-park side?'

'Mah?' Stink offers me the disgusting, spit-encrusted train.

'Bleurgh,' I say to him, sticking out my tongue.

'Mo says, no thanks, Ewan!' Dad makes his voice all singsong and irritating.

'So, which side?'

'Huh?' I get up from the table and put my bowl in the sink.

'The park? Carys' house?'

'Oh, I don't remember. Somewhere in the middle, I think. Brushing teeth.' I mime the gesture to Stink who waves his train happily, narrowly missing whacking himself on the nose.

I escape up the stairs and breathe. I am rubbish at lying. I know I can't tell Dad where we went as he will be so mad, but it makes me feel like there is a layer of mud on my words and he will just be able to see through what I say and know.

We went to Denham. Me and Onyx. We did something no one else in our year has dared to do, and we have promised each other that we are going to go back, as soon as we can.

I feel a rush thinking about it. Going into school seems so much easier today, like I'm braver than all of them. Ellie and Maya don't matter anymore. I've got Onyx.

'Why don't you invite Carys over for tea?' Diane says, peering through the open bathroom door.

I mutter non-committally through my toothpaste. I could invite Onyx here, but our friendship feels like something I want to keep separate from home for now, though I can't explain why.

Onyx is sitting on the wall by the school gates near the big kids when I walk up the drive. She jumps off and saunters over to me, linking her arm through mine.

'Hey, bestie.'

'Hey, how good was that yesterday? I was thinking, I'm going to go to the library and see if I can find any plans of the building. Maybe we can work out where we should search next?' I say as we start to wander over in the direction of form room.

'Maybe.'

'I really want to tell Mr Brock. I bet he'd be really interested, y'know?' I say.

'No,' Onyx says firmly. 'Not a good idea, Mo. He's an adult; he'll just tell our folks and we'll be grounded.'

'Yeah. Oh yeah, probably. I've never been grounded. It's a weird phrase, isn't it? Like, what do they do to you?'

'Grind you into dust!'

'Oh yeah. Nasty.' We grin at each other.

The bell goes and we join the mass of moving kids.

'Losers, move out the way.' Ellie and her crew flock past, all elbows and flicky ponytails.

Normally I never stand up to Ellie. Normally I just

let her carry on with her nasty comments. But I've had enough. 'Stop calling us losers,' I mutter.

'Er, why? You are,' Ellie snorts as she jostles into the front of the queue. 'Emo and—' She looks me up and down like I'm some giant grey bogey, deliberately leaving her sentence hanging.

Sometimes I really hate her. 'We're braver than you any day.'

'Mo.' Onyx nudges me and pulls at my arm, but I am too full of our adventure and sick of Ellie. I'm not the same person I was yesterday and I'm not going to listen to her nasty little comments anymore.

'Whatever!' Ellie pauses and laughs. 'So?'

'We went to the old asylum yesterday. Right inside.'

'You never,' Maya dismisses us.

'We did. I got pictures.' I get out my phone and show them the one of Onyx at the top of the staircase.

'It's against the law to go in there,' Ellie says, changing tack.

'Just 'cause you haven't got the guts,' Onyx says, deciding to back me up.

'Not stupid enough.' Ellie flicks her hair, but her eyes have changed shape somehow.

'Wooah, did you really go?' Sambhav grabs my arm to look at the picture on my phone. 'Awesome. Lads, Mo's been in the asylum.'

'Me and Onyx.' I beam.

I hear one of the wannabes snorting about the name Onyx, but I'm busy concentrating on showing the pictures to Sambhav, Mylo and Harry.

'What was it like?' Mylo asks.

'Cool,' Onyx takes over. 'We're going back.'

'Yeah?' Sambhav looks impressed.

'We're going to find the treatment rooms too,' I explain.

'And we're gonna do it at night.' Onyx grins at me, her eyes glittering.

'At night?' I mutter. 'Who said that? Why at night?'

'Oh, just to shut them up.' Onyx nods to the rest of the class as they flood into form room in front of us.

I sit down and get out my planner, not saying anything, pretending I'm looking at the timetable. I can't see the point of going at night. It was hard enough to see in the daylight. It just seems a stupid dare-type thing. A silly sort of thing Sambhav and the others would say to each other. I don't know how to say this to Onyx, though. I thought she understood. I'm not sure how I put into words the discomfort I feel at the idea.

Geography is okay, but then it's science and there is a new seating plan.

'I don't see why I have to sit back here with *you*,'

Ellie says huffily, as she dumps her bag and pencil case down. She's got one of those furry ones with a giant pink ball that you pull to open the zip.

I move my stuff to make way for her, trying to think up a suitable insult, but miss my moment, as usual.

We are *still* on classification. Apparently, there is a test in a week so we go over the stuff we've already done. Double boring. Don't worry, though, I learnt my lesson and know not to say anything in case Mr Jones has a tantrum.

Ellie is busy getting all her different highlighters out and underlining in different colours. I try to ignore her tutting and clicking, but then—

'So, you and Carys are best mates now then?' Click, she pushes on a pen lid and nods in Onyx's direction.

I shrug.

'Oh, I forgot, silly me. It's Onyx now, right?'

I don't reply.

'I mean, why change your name? What's that all about?' She puts a flourish of peach around the table we've drawn in our books.

'I like it,' I say.

Mr Jones gives us both a cross look and Ellie goes quiet for a minute, then—

'Mmm,' Ellie murmurs. 'Is she gay then? A they/them?'

'No … I—' I don't actually know why Onyx doesn't like her name and if she's gay or not. It doesn't make any difference to me. Onyx is Onyx. I'm just wondering how to explain this when Ellie butts into my thoughts.

'If you want my opinion, Carys is just attention-seeking.' Ellie writes the word *kingdom* into her table, adding a heart over the 'i' instead of a dot.

'Huh?'

'Goth hair, freaky name and now she's dragged you into her little scheme. I mean, going to the asylum, Mo, really? She's using you.'

Another glance from Mr Jones, but I'm getting cross now. What does she mean Onyx is using me?

'It was my idea,' I say through gritted teeth as I write down the next answer. 'Going to Denham was my idea.'

Ellie's snort induces a 'QUIET!' from Mr Jones. I ignore Ellie's attempts to try and get me to talk again and soon enough it's breaktime.

It gets round the school pretty quickly that we've been to Denham. A couple of the older kids nod at us in the yard. I'm too surprised to say anything, but Onyx gives a little grin at one of them. I'm itching to go to the library to look at plans, but Onyx has persuaded me they won't have anything. 'You need to check online. And DON'T let your mum and dad see what you're looking at. They might guess.'

What Ellie said is like a fly buzzing about in a trapped jar. Why would Onyx be using me?

'So, why did you say we should go to Denham in the dark?'

'Huh?'

'To Sambhav. You said—'

'Oh, right. I just thought it sounded more outrageous!'

'Why do we need to be outrageous? I don't think we'll see well if we go in the dark. I want to be able to see what's there.'

'You scared?' Onyx asks. I can't see her expression because of her fringe but I don't like the tone of her voice. It sounds a bit, well, it sounds a bit like Ellie – teasing me.

'Scared?' I've crossed my arms.

'You know of the dark, ghosts. Oooh!' She comes at me doing zombie arms, but turns her attack into a hug. It feels too rough though and not like a hug should.

'No. Ghosts aren't real. I don't mind the dark, but it just seems a bit ... well ... a bit stupid to go in the dark.'

'I just thought it sounded more fun.' Onyx shrugs and quits the zombie-ghost impression.

‘Is that a peopling thing – doing something stupid because it sounds fun?’ I scratch my head.

Onyx laughs. ‘What?’

‘Like what other people do – normal people. I don’t always get it.’

‘Probably,’ she says, linking arms with me and giving my arm a squeeze.

I’m quiet for a moment, then, ‘Why do you want to go back? I mean why did you want to go at all?’

‘Huh?’

‘To the asylum?’

‘You asked me, remember?’ Onyx bashes my arm playfully.

‘Yeah, I guess.’ I grin and try to forget about Ellie and her stupid ideas.

FRIDAY 24 SEPTEMBER

'Mum, what's an attention-seeker?' I ask, as I try and fail for the third time to do up my tie.

'It's someone who deliberately goes out of their way to get people to pay attention to them – usually by acting in more dramatic ways. Like Nev.' Mum directs the last comment at Nev who is pretending to do up a tie and strangling himself with it.

'I'm not an attention-seeker!' he says, dropping the act and coming over to help me.

'No, not really, you're just a numpty,' she says, kissing him.

'Seriously!' I complain. Why do adults always do the sharing saliva thing?

'I guess attention-seekers often don't feel recognised. Yes, I guess they feel invisible?' Mum says, zipping up my school bag. I can tell she is getting into this discussion, though, because she's stopped worrying about the time. 'So, they try to get attention, any kind, even if it is bad attention – to kind of make up for it?'

'Is dying your hair and changing your name attention-seeking then?' I ask.

'Not necessarily, MoMo. Growing up makes people want to explore their identity and find out who they are. They aren't just who their parents say they are anymore. Fashion and dress sense all come out of identity. Did you know I died my hair green when I was sixteen?'

'Doesn't surprise me,' Nev quips.

'I bet you've never changed, have you?' Mum calls back. 'You were born with short back and sides and your nose in an astrophysics book.'

'Maybe.'

I tug my coat on.

'Done!' Mum beams, throwing her phone into her bag. 'Come on then. See you.' She kisses Nev again and sweeps me out of the door with her. 'So, who is the attention-seeker? Is this the new friend Dad said you'd made? What's her name?'

'Carys – but she prefers Onyx, only don't tell her mum and dad that.'

'Alright.' Mum is silent for a moment. 'And who thinks she's an attention-seeker?'

'Ellie said—'

Mum snorts with laughter. 'Ellie's the biggest attention-seeker I know! I would take what she says with a pinch of salt.'

'Pinch of salt?'

'It just means – well, don't believe everything she says.'

'Oh, right.'

'Look, there's one way to know. Invite Onyx over and I'll be able to tell you what I think!'

'Oh, Mum,' I groan.

'Come on! I want to meet her.'

'I'll think about it.'

At the end of the day, I have maths. Miss Pool sends me out of most lessons now. I even have a desk outside the classroom and am tempted to just go and sit there before she has a chance to attack. I sit as still as I can, trying not to tap my feet.

'There will be no talking today. We have an assessment.'

All we do is assessments.

We are being assessed on adding negative numbers to positive ones. The problem is that I don't have the number line in my book, because I got sent out last lesson for sneezing.

I can't ask her for help because she will eat me.

I write the title and the date. I underline with a ruler. I indent my paragraphs and … *STRIKE.*

'Maureen. I told you to write "Negative Number Assessment" as the title.'

'I didn't realise.'

'That's because you don't listen. You never listen. Get your things.'

She holds the door open for me with her scaly hands. The vicious nails tapping the wood impatiently.

I drag my bag, pencil case and book and head out, but the pencil case slips from my grasp and falls. I stop to pick up the pens that have spilt out. Miss Pool stands there waiting.

'Is everything okay, Miss Pool? Mo?' a familiar voice asks.

I look up to see Ms Latimer, but she is already bending down to help me pick up my things, placing them on the table as she does so.

'Oh dear. Why are you outside?' she asks me directly.

I glance at Miss Pool, uncertain what to say.

'Maureen finds it difficult to work in the class. She is better concentrating out here.'

'Oh dear. Really? I've always found her concentration is excellent! Hasn't the school changed the name on the register yet, Mo?' Ms Latimer asks me.

I shake my head, my pointless mouth unable to speak.

'I'll get on to it now. I'm going to see the head, so I'll do it on my way.' Ms Latimer directs this at Miss

Pool, who nods slightly and shuts the door, leaving me in the corridor.

Ms Latimer doesn't walk away from the classroom, though. She kneels next to my chair and speaks quietly. 'Has Miss Pool sent you out here before, Mo?'

I hesitate, not knowing what to say and whether I can trust my mouth to speak.

'It's okay. You're not in trouble.'

I nod.

'More than once?'

I nod again.

She frowns and looks about to speak further, but instead stands up again. 'Okay. Well, you do your best, okay, and don't worry.' She pats me lightly on the shoulder and walks along the corridor toward the head's office.

SATURDAY 25 SEPTEMBER

Ellie's broken her arm in two places. The class group chat's been set back up again and I've been added, but I think she's only done it to get sympathy. She's taken a picture of her bright red cast. Everyone is sending sympathetic emojis.

Apparently, she landed badly in training on Friday night. She'll be out of training for at least six weeks, but it could be up to three months. I am tempted to put a laughing face, but I don't. My thumb hovers over it for a second, but I don't message anything. I'll pretend I never saw it. Maybe now she'll know what missing out feels like.

I take a critical look around my room.

Onyx is coming over later. Mum insisted. If I was normal, it would probably make me have a good feeling, but I'm not normal and I feel sick. I don't want anyone in my room, in my space. I look around thinking what I should hide so I don't get teased. I move my blanket right away and stuff it in a box under my bed.

Once I've kind of tidied myself away, I power up my PC and start to look for asylum floor plans. I can't find any at all. I'm so engrossed in the search I don't hear the door and the first I know that Onyx has arrived is Mum shouting my name. There is a short knock on my door. Then Onyx is here. In my room.

'Hey!' Onyx looks like Onyx today. She's got her hair how she likes it and is wearing all black. She's got rings on too, and a pendant with a star on it. 'Oh my GOD, Mo, I love your room.' She wanders over to the mural and reaches out a hand to it. She doesn't touch it but traces the snow leopard with a finger in the air. 'Who did this? It's amazing!'

I'm distracted because she is wearing shoes on my carpet and I hate anyone wearing shoes on my carpet. Mum should've told her to take her shoes off. I'm struggling with how to say it when Mum taps on my door and looks in.

'Hey! I'm just having a cuppa with your mum downstairs, Carys. You two want a drink?'

'No thanks,' Onyx and me say together. Mum catches my eye and straightaway she knows.

'Carys, love, would you mind taking your shoes off when you're upstairs? I'll take them down and leave them in the hall. It's just the carpets – you know.' Mum laughs lightly.

'Oh sorry! I should have remembered.' Onyx slips the shoes off and hands them to Mum.

'No worries. Shout if you need anything!'

Mum goes with the shoes and I can breathe.

'Mum did it.' I point to the mural. 'I love it too.'

'Hey, what's your favourite animal? I've got this app and it tells you your spirit creature.' Onyx flops on my bed next to me, which feels a bit weird, but I can cope with it. Before long I forget all about it feeling weird as we start to laugh about the fact Onyx got starfish as her spirit creature and the time just flies.

MONDAY 27 SEPTEMBER

I really need the toilet. Luckily the English teacher, Mrs Gerrard, is quite nice and lets me go.

I hate going to the school toilets, but at least in lesson time they are usually quiet. Sometimes older students hide in them though and Onyx said some were vaping in there last week. Anyway, there's no one in here, thank goodness.

I yank my pants down to pee and it looks like I've pooed myself! But it's in the wrong place. Using tissue I wipe most of it off but then, once I pee, I wipe myself and there's more of it. It's not poo, it's blood! I've started my period. Why did no one tell me period blood looks brown! Mum packed a sanitary towel in my school bag ages ago, but I didn't bring my bag with me. I don't know what to do. I'm taking ages and Mrs Gerrard is going to be cross when I get back. I stuff some tissue in my pants and flush. Then when I go and wash my hands, I see there is a stack of sanitary towels by the sinks. I grab one and go and sort myself out.

It feels all weird. I've got cramps and I can feel the sticky wet feeling and then the scratchy pad between my legs. I HATE GROWING UP!

Maths is weird too. There is another teacher at the back of Miss Pool's class today making notes. And Miss Pool is almost nice to me. She moves me to the front in the middle and stuffs Ellie in my old seat. Ellie complains about having to move, but even she doesn't make too much fuss in Miss Pool's class. I can finally see the board! I'm also sat next to Sambhav who, though he can be very annoying, is happy to help me copy when I'm being too slow to get things off the board. Even though I don't finish the work, I don't get shouted at or kept behind during break. Result!

When I tell Mum I've started my period, she gives me this cute squirrel-pattern pouch to keep my towels in, and I get extra pudding. She goes on about the importance of changing my pads regularly, until I start yawning and she leaves me alone.

TUESDAY 28 SEPTEMBER

'My mum wants you to come over for tea on Thursday,' Onyx says, as she kicks her legs against the wall.

I'm busy catching up with homework that's due in, leaning my book on the bricks and trying not to scrawl too much. Something in her tone makes me wonder whether Onyx wants me to come over or just her mum. Is this like it was with Ellie? Our mum's putting all the effort in when really Ellie didn't like me at all?

'Do *you* want me to come for tea tomorrow?' I ask, trying to read her expression.

'Yeah, course. It's just, well – my dad might be home.'

'Ah. The piranha food.'

'Yep. Exactly. Your mum was so cool and Nev was really friendly and my parents aren't like that at all. They're – I can't explain it – just so … stiff!' She throws her arms open dramatically. 'Hopefully he'll be out. He's a consultant so goes to different hospitals.'

I have a lumpy feeling when I think about Onyx's dad, like I have a party of rocks in my stomach. I do not think he likes me at all.

'Lara's down there.' I point with my pen changing the subject.

This part of school has become our favourite place to hang out. I think I know why Onyx likes coming here the most, because sometimes Lara and her friends hang out down near the car park to skateboard. I like it because it is quiet and you never get smacked by accidental footballs flying about.

'I know. Did you know she's – they're – gender fluid?'

'Gender what?'

'Really, Mo?'

Mum's taught me the word for the expression on Onyx's face right now. It's called exasperated. 'What?' I say. 'I don't know what it is. She doesn't want to be a girl or something?'

'No. It means like, they don't always feel like a girl, and they don't always feel like a boy. They kind of feel both and neither.'

'It sounds confusing.'

'It's not. It's easy. You sometimes use they/them pronouns.'

'Oh, right. I know about them.' I nod. I used

to watch this YouTuber who cut all their hair and started using they/them. 'Even more stuff for me to get wrong by the sounds of it.' I shut my English book and put my pen away. 'Hang on, Lara's heading this way.'

'Are they? Oh my God. Don't look.' Onyx turns toward me and fluffs up her hair.

'Hey.' Lara smiles at us as they wander past.

'Hey.' Onyx turns just in time to catch their smile.

'You really like Lara, don't you?'

'No!' Onyx whacks me on the arm.

'What was that for?' I rub the place where she smacked me.

'I don't like them like that.'

'Like what? Huh? You're peopling again and I don't understand!' I cry.

'Forget it. Come on, it's your fave subject.' She grabs my bag and helps haul me off the wall.

'Because asylums were so crowded and subject to abuse, other forms of extreme medical treatment began to be used. Has anyone heard of a lobotomy?' Mr Brock asks the class.

'That's what Leo's had,' Mylo says, under his breath. A few people snigger.

'That will get you a detention, Mylo, thank you.

Let's not get offensive.' Mr Brock stares at Mylo who stops laughing and looks at his feet.

I know the answer because I saw it on one of the websites. Onyx nudges me to put my hand up. 'Go on, Mo, tell them.' It is the only lesson apart from HWE where we're sat together.

I put my hand up half-heartedly. I don't think Mr Brock is going to get annoyed with me, but I never know these days.

'Mo?'

'A lobotomy was an operation that was performed on mental patients. Doctors used to cut part of the brain away while they were still awake.'

'Yes.' Mr Brock beams at me. 'Did it work, do you think?'

'Well, they sometimes did, but only because they turned the patients into vegetables.'

Mr Brock laughed. 'True. They were very inaccurate and crude ways of dealing with problems such as schizophrenia. But people thought that better than filling asylums full to the brim and having to restrain people and stick them in padded cells.'

Mr Brock shows us some pictures and writing of other kinds of Victorian 'cures'. We work in pairs to put them in order of reliability. There are extracts from newspapers, old photos, letters and a list of names. The handwritten ones are really hard to read, the words are curled up like they've shrivelled with time.

'Sources are so valuable to a historian,' Mr Brock says excitedly, when we've finished. 'There are sources from places like newspapers, but there are also local sources, like those extracts from personal letters.' He points to the ones I can't read. 'And those from the local library. There's a great local-history section there,' he raises his voice to be heard above the bell and the noise of people starting to pack away, 'if anyone's interested.'

THURSDAY 30 SEPTEMBER

'Hello, Mo.' Onyx's mum smiles at us, as we clamber into the back of the Land Rover. 'I'm Nina. Nice to meet you again. Did you both have a good day?'

'It is now we're leaving school,' Onyx says.

I just smile. The seats feel slippery and the belts are giant clunky things that make a good click when you put them on.

'How was the test?'

'Awful. I did the test and only got seven out of twenty. Everyone else did better than me.' Onyx reaches into the seat pocket and unearths some fruit pastilles that she offers me.

'I only got nine. And the highest in the class was eleven. Mrs Gerrard said it was a really hard test,' I explain.

Onyx shrugs and stuffs a pastille in her mouth.

'Are you enjoying school?' Onyx's mum asks.

I put my head on one side. 'Some of it.'

'I like science,' Onyx says.

'Eww no! Mr Jones is rubbish.' I still haven't

forgiven him for my lunchtime detention in my first week.

'He's funny.'

'He's an idiot. At least Mr Brock knows something. Mr Jones doesn't know a fish from a falafel!'

Onyx snorts with laughter.

'Carys!' Her mum admonishes. She pulls the Land Rover into the drive. There is a blue BMW parked in front of a big detached redbrick house. Autumnal trees are waving about and there is a neat lawn with flowerbeds around the edges.

'God. Dad's home.' Onyx is staring at the blue car. Her whole body has gone sort of still.

'Yes, the operation in Sheffield he was overseeing was cancelled so he's back early,' Onyx's mum says, in a brittle, cheerful tone as she parks beside the other car.

'Great. I'll kill myself now, shall I?' Onyx flings herself back in the seat and crosses her arms.

'Don't be like that. He's away next week for five days. There's a neurosurgeon's conference in London. It'll be okay.'

Onyx glowers out of the window, not speaking.

There is a big fat wedge of tension in the car, so I get out my planner and start looking through the homework that we've been set so far this week.

‘Come on, Carys,’ her mum says in a firmer voice, getting out of the car and opening Onyx’s door. ‘Be a good host and show Mo around. There’s some fresh shortbread in the kitchen.’

Reluctantly Onyx clambers out of the Land Rover, holding the door for me. We drag our bags after us and I follow into the house.

The porch has pretty black and white tiles and all the shoes are arranged tidily on racks. We all take our shoes off before going through a second door into the house.

There is a hallway with doors leading off it and a grandfather clock ticking loudly.

‘Woah, your house is massive.’

‘These were nineteenth-century merchants’ houses,’ Onyx’s mum explains. ‘They were rather grand at the time. Why don’t you show Mo your room, Carys? There is a great view over the town. I’m going to start dinner.’

Onyx heaves her bag over her shoulder and indicates for me to follow. There is a first flight of stairs with a lovely wooden twisting banister that feels smooth under my palms. The landing is massive and there are a load more doors. At the end is a second staircase leading up again. Onyx treads up, sighing.

At the top there are two doors. Onyx opens one and ushers me inside, shutting the door behind me.

It is a beautiful room, painted all white with a double bed in the centre. There is a giant desk on one side and a big Narnia cupboard on the other. Pretty drop lights hang from the beamed ceiling.

'Fancy!' I say, dumping my bag on the floor.

'It's so old fashioned,' Onyx says, throwing her bag with some force against the desk. 'I'm not allowed to paint the walls. I'm not allowed to put pictures up. I'm not even allowed to Blu Tack things on.' She rolls on the bed and slaps her hand over her eyes.

I sit next to her, still drinking in the place. It reminds me of a hotel room. It is all lovely, but I can't see anything of Onyx here.

'Have you got any clothes with you?' she sits up suddenly.

'Huh?' I look down at my uniform. 'I'm wearing some.'

'No, I mean to change in to.'

'Er, no.'

'Dad won't let me sit at the table unless I've changed.' Her mouth twists and she raises her eyebrows.

'Seriously?'

'Yep.'

'He probably won't freak out about you wearing your uniform.' She bites at her fingernail. 'But you could borrow something of mine, I guess.' She opens the wardrobe and there are rows of brightly coloured clothes, neatly ironed and hung up.

I look through them. Hoodies, leggings. The kinds of things Ellie would wear, not Onyx. Branded stuff. T-shirts with bright designs: Surf's Up, Team USA and Nike. There is a green hoodie near the back that has a little tree logo on it. I pick it out.

'I've never even worn that! I got it from camp two years ago. It might not even fit you.'

'I'm a bit smaller than you.' We stand next to each other comparing. Onyx is half a head taller than me.

I pull off my school tie, cardigan and blouse.

'A vest, Mo?!'

'So? Don't look! I get cold,' I say, as I drag the hoodie over my head. The jumper fits okay. It smells of lavender and cupboards, but the label pokes into my neck. I drag it off. 'Eww! Sorry – no. I can't wear it. It is too—' I shake my hands, 'Scratchy.' I put my shirt and tie back on.

The vest also covers my stupid sprouting boobs. I am not ready to wear a bra yet. I refuse to change my skirt. 'What is your dad going to do to me?'

'Probably nothing,' Onyx says. 'He just saves it all up for me.'

'Oh my God! Does he hurt you?'

'No but it's all: No TV. No laptop. No dessert. No allowance. No breathing... He is a fascist.' Onyx pulls on a red Just Do It! hoodie and some colourful leggings. 'I have to fake everything when he's home. This is my real wardrobe.' She grabs a large plastic box from under her bed. Inside are black jeans and T-shirts. There is a purple hoodie with a skull on it and another with a wolf staring at a giant moon. 'But apparently *girls* shouldn't wear black. It's *morbid*.'

'What century is he from? I love this,' I say, picking up the wolf hoodie.

'I know. He has no idea. I do really hate him.' She pulls off her jewellery and throws it in with the clothes, then shoves the box back under her bed with force.

'Come on. I'll show you round—'

'OH MY GOD! You can see Denham from here.' I point excitedly out of the window.

'Yeah, just the roof, I guess.' Onyx stands next to me and looks out.

'Did you know they used to think autism was a mental illness? And that they could cure gayness? Doctors used to use electric shock treatment to abuse their patients and parents used to pay for their kids to have it done.' I mime electricity fizzing through my body. 'I wonder if they did ECT at Denham.'

'Why isn't it called EST?' Onyx says, as she drags a brush half-heartedly through her hair.

'Oh. ECT – Electro Convulsive Therapy. But most people say Electric Shock Tr—'

'I think my dad would use those treatments now if he could,' Onyx says, interrupting. 'Come on, come see the rest of the house and we'll find the shortbread.'

There are two knives and spoons and cloth napkins. It's like the posh hotel we stayed in when Mum married Nev. Onyx sits opposite me, silent.

Onyx's dad is at the top of the table and hasn't said a word to me yet. He has Miss Pool vibes. I'm just wondering if they're related, when Onyx's mum appears carrying some bowls with soup in.

'Thanks,' I say and sniff the soup. It is something chickeny. I dip the bread in and take a slurp. It's okay, but needs salt.

'Ahem.' Onyx's dad is frowning at me. 'We say grace first before we eat in this house.'

'Oh sorry.' I plop my wet bread on the side plate and wait.

I listen to them say a prayer with my hands on my lap, looking politely out of the window.

When they finish, we all begin our soup. Her dad

looks at me. 'Do your family not expect you to change for your evening meal?'

'Oh no,' I explain, as I resume my exploration of the soup. Mum will be really proud of me for trying something new. 'We just wear what we want. I can't be bothered changing out of my uniform.' I smile and dip my bread in my soup.

Onyx's mum clears her throat. 'What is your favo—'

'This is what the issue is these days,' George, Onyx's dad says, laying his spoon tidily next to his bowl and patting his mouth. 'Young people have a "can't be bothered" attitude about everything.'

'Has everyone finished the soup?' Onyx's mum asks.

I wipe my mouth with the napkin in case I have a soup beard. 'Thank you. I actually liked that!' I say, handing her the bowl.

'How are you finding school, Mo?' she asks, as she collects the bowls together.

'I hate most of it,' I say. 'The maths teacher hates me and is always keeping me in for no reason, but it is better than the first week when Ellie lied and told the science teacher I'd pushed her over and I ended up in a lunchtime detention. But history is good and I like drama club and making friends with Carys.' I smile to show I've finished talking.

'You've had a detention already!' George looks disbelievingly at his wife. 'You've been in secondary school less than a month!'

'My dad says some teachers are just autocrats on a power trip and that I just need to keep being myself and not worry about it.'

'Does he now? Does he not teach you to respect your elders? That punishment is given for a reason?'

'Mum says, adults ought to earn respect, not just—' I feel something touch my foot under the chair and instinctively look under the tablecloth. It is Onyx trying to kick me from the other side of the table. She's frowning at me. '...Not just be given respect when they don't deserve it.'

'Really! In this house, we believe in a little more respect and a lot less rudeness. Nina, I will finish my meal in the study.' And with that, Onyx's dad pushes his chair back and stands. 'As soon as she has finished her meal, Nina, please take her home.'

'Oh gawd,' Onyx says, putting her hands over her face.

Silence stretches like chewing gum as we all stare at the door he just pulled shut behind him.

'Sorry. I've offended your dad. I didn't mean to,' I say, feeling my cheeks getting hot. 'I did really, really like the soup.'

'It's not you,' Onyx hisses. 'He is so embarrassing! I should've warned you to avoid conversations about anything negative.'

'It'll be fine. I'll just go and get the main course,' Nina says, heading out of the dining room, but the expression on her face does not look like it is fine.

And even though Onyx says I didn't do anything wrong, I can't shake the feeling I've just made a big mistake.

'So, what was it like?' Dad asks as he ties a stinky nappy bag and plops it in the bin.

'Excruciating,' I say, flopping onto the sofa next to Diane and Stink.

'Why was it bad, MoMo?' Diane asks in a stupid baby voice, jiggling Stink's arms up and down.

I frown at her, taking Stink off her and putting him on my knee. He's just had his bath and is all clean and nice smelling. 'Hello Stinky.' I give him a cuddle. Stink gurgles at me and bats at my mouth with his hand, grinning.

'Carys' dad is like a sergeant major. They call tea, dinner, and had three courses. We had to say a prayer before we ate and then I had a discussion with George, that's Onyx's dad, about respect. But he ended up going to eat somewhere else. I think I offended him.'

'Oh, Mo,' Dad says, ruffling my hair.

'I know! I feel sorry for Ony– I mean Carys. It's all so strict.'

'You wonder why some people have kids,' Diane says, stroking the nape of Stink's neck with her forefinger and making him giggle. He's gone all sleepy and soft against me and it feels lovely.

'Her mum's okay, but just does everything Onyx's dad says.'

'I thought he looked a bit weird at Blue Zoo,' Dad offers.

'He's not weird. He's mean.'

'True. You're weird but lovely.' Dad reaches over and ruffles my hair.

'Stop,' I say. 'You'll wake Stink.'

And for the first time in ages, we all just sit together and watch some crappage on the TV. Diane lets Stink stay sleeping on me instead of whisking him off to his crib, and I'm glad my families are the way they are – imperfect and messy. I think of poor Onyx in that huge, still house and wish I could rescue her.

FRIDAY 1 OCTOBER

Posters have appeared around the school for auditions for the school show. They are doing *Barnabas and the Circus of Dreams.*

Onyx isn't in school again, and even though I message her I get no reply. I have this ugly space in my stomach worrying about what happened at her house. Will she even want to talk to me now after the way I talked to her dad?

I trudge over to drama club because it's Friday and that's the routine. As I walk through the door, Sambhav pounces on me and shouts in my ear, 'On freeedom's side!', which is one of the more famous songs from the show.

'Stop it,' I say, putting down my bag.

'You putting your name down?' Sambhav points to the list everyone is crowding round. They're holding auditions next week.

'Maybe.' I wander over to the group gathering about Ms Latimer's table. Lara and their friend are trying to stop people pushing but it's too busy and I can't get near it. I can't sing so don't really think there's much point in me auditioning. I try to remember the main part – there is Barnabas, obviously, then all the different characters in the *freak* show. Not that we'd call it that now. I remember the tightrope walker one was pretty cool, but I'm sure she sings a solo.

'Ms Latimer isn't here today, but you can still put your names down if you like. The auditions will be next week,' Lara says to the people coming in.

'Oh, I already have,' Ellie exclaims. 'I've put my name down for Barnabas, obviously, but my sister says that the main parts go to the GCSE students, so I've put my name down for the artists too.' Ellie bats another girl away from her, using her cast.

'OW! Careful,' the girl shouts.

Lara's friend with the moustache hands her the list sniggering. 'You can't put your name down for ALL the parts, Ellie!'

Lara wafts the paper about. 'RIGHT, listen everyone. I'll tell you a bit about the script and that might help you decide who you want to audition for. I reckon two parts max?'

They look at the other exam students who nod agreement.

'So, there is Barnabas who is the main one. It's unlikely any of you will get the main part unless you are super-amazing.' They avoid Ellie's smug nodding face. 'Then there are all the performers. They are all kind of similar in the amount of time they have on the stage. It's different from the film because they each have their own back story. Colin and Rosemary – that's the posh guy and the singer – they have a bit more to say because of the love interest. The rival circus owner is quite a big part – he's Billy Whizz. Then there's Barnabas' family, who are at the start and end of the play.'

'And the chorus.' The other student chips in.

'Oh yeah, if you just fancy singing and a bit of dancing, stick your name down for the chorus.'

People crowd around the list once more, Ellie pointedly rubbing out her name from most of the parts.

I'm wondering about whether I should eat my sandwich in here or not as the club isn't really on today, when Lara comes over to me.

'Hey, bug. Are you putting your name down?'

'I can't sing. There's no point.' I shrug.

'I'm not a natural singer either but Mr Kaspar, the music teacher, can give you a bit of voice coaching. And if you're a really good actor there will be ways round it.' Lara grins at me. 'And what about your little buddy?'

'She's not in today.'

'Well, you can at least put your names down to help backstage? That's the lighting and scenery and stuff.'

'Yeah, okay,' I say, more to please them than any other reason. I really want to ask them about what it feels like to be gender fluid, but I'm guessing that isn't a conversation for now.

'So, the list will be up until Wednesday next week for you to put your names down, okay?' they say to everyone, and then they move away to talk to Sambhav.

I wish Onyx was here. I miss her and haven't spoken to her since I was at her house. I decide not to put my name down after all and slope off to hang out in the library.

MONDAY 4 OCTOBER

Mum's picking me up tonight. I love being at Dad's, but at the end of a five-day stretch I really miss Mum. I talk to her on the phone and everything, but it's not the same.

I'm walking up to the school entrance when hands cover my eyes from behind. 'Boo!' Onyx shouts.

'Don't do that!' I snap crossly, as I slap her hands away.

'What's wrong?' Her face looks a bit shocked.

'I don't like surprises,' I say, calming down as I see her face. 'You didn't know. I just get really – itchy – when people do that to me. I'm the same with tickling.'

'Itchy?' Onyx's face passes from upset to amused.

'Yes, itchy. Don't you ever get that? You know, when you just feel like—' I jump about a bit trying to show her what I mean. '…Like your skin is prickling on the inside.'

'Um.' She makes a thinking face. 'No.'

'Sorry. I'm okay with hugs?' I say, opening my arms to her.

'I do hugs,' she says, and it is the first time we hug.

'Where were you on Friday? You've missed three Fridays,' I say, as we settle down into form room. It isn't 9 a.m. yet, so we can chat. 'I was worried after that meal at your house. I didn't mean to upset your dad.'

She snorts. 'Don't worry. Everything upsets my dad. He makes me go to a psychiatrist on Fridays. He thinks I can be fixed.' Onyx says this in the usual tone she uses when she speaks about her dad, sarcastic and hard sounding.

'Fixed? But there's nothing wrong with you.'

'Oh well, according to him, there's lots.'

'How're the emos today?' Ellie bustles over to us. She's replaced her rucksack from the start of term with a gold handbag and has it slung over her good arm. Even though she's come over and is talking to us, she is scanning the room as though looking for a better option. It's then I notice Maya and the wannabes are here, huddled together by the radiator. They glance over at Ellie but there are no smiles.

Onyx looks at me and I shrug imperceptibly.

'I mean, what's going on?' Ellie sits in front of us like she is staying.

'Well, we were talking about the emo meeting we're going to later. Wanna come? Interested?' Onyx says, nudging my foot with hers under the table.

'Oh yeah. Come along. You'll have to get the clothes, though. I mean...' I look her up and down, like she always does us, as though we've smeared ourselves in doggy doodoo.

'Seriously? I never knew that you had meetings?' She shuffles uncomfortably in her chair, holding her handbag between us like a guard.

'Oh yeah. It's a national thing. We've got a flag – haven't you seen the monochrome rainbow?' says Onyx.

I start to snigger then. I can't help it. Ellie just believes every word.

'Oh my God. You're joking, right?' She laughs loud and fake. 'I knew that.'

'What was all that about?' I mouth at Onyx when Ellie turns away.

'Trouble in paradise,' Onyx replies, nodding in Maya's direction.

Mr Pebbles, the head of year, pops his head into the classroom. A few kids are staring at him. He only usually appears if someone's in trouble. 'Carys, could I speak to you outside?' He smiles briefly. 'You're not in trouble. Bring your stuff.' He gestures to her bag and coat. Onyx looks completely bewildered. I watch as she leaves the form room and does not come back.

At breaktime, I rush to the wall to see if Onyx is there. I don't know whether she's gone home or not. She can't be in exclusion, because Mr Pebbles said she wasn't in trouble.

I'm just about to give up when Onyx appears around the corner of the maths building.

'Where did you go?' I ask.

She slams her bag onto the floor. 'I've been moved classes, to 7B.' Her eyes are wet with tears. 'Mr Pebbles said my dad insisted or he is going to take me out of this school. I'm so mad! He is trying to control my whole life.'

I don't know what to do or say, so I just put my arms around her.

After a few moments she sits back on the wall. Her eyes all puffy and wet.

'Is this because of me, because of the respect thing?' Shame soaks through me when I see the expression on Onyx's face. 'Why do I always say the wrong thing? I just can't people.' It's my turn to feel mad. Mad at myself for being so weird and useless.

'He said last night that I should be going to a church school. That I need positive influences around me. He thinks he can make me grow into this person who he wants me to be. He can't just let me be myself.'

'You'll make new friends in 7B,' I say staring at my twitchy feet.

'He can't stop me being friends with you.' She grabs my arm and squeezes it. 'And he can't stop me being who I really am, however hard he tries.'

TUESDAY 5 OCTOBER

Morning form time is weird and empty without Onyx. Ellie sits by me again and completely ignores Maya and the others, though now I think I know why.

Now Onyx and I are in totally different classes, we've agreed the wall is going to be our meeting place. I hurry over there at breaktime and she's already there looking glum.

'I hate 7B,' she complains. 'There are some really mean kids in there and I STILL get Miss Pool for maths.'

'That's rubbish,' I say sympathetically.

'How was Smelly Ellie today?' she asks.

'Oh yes. That reminds me.' I take my phone out of my pocket. We aren't supposed to have them out in school and, if a teacher sees, I could get it confiscated. I'm one of those weird people who likes rules but I will break them if it's important, and knowledge is always important, right?

I open the chat to show Onyx. 'There was a comp on this weekend.'

'Comp?' she quizzes.

'Gymnastics competition.'

'Oh, I forgot you used to do that.'

'I think I know why they've fallen out.' I look up and show my phone screen to Onyx:

Maya386 I got a gold!

Ells010 Wow!! Amazing Maya.

Hope they didn't miss me too much

Maya386 I've been picked for national tryouts!!!!

Ells010 Seriously? I didn't know they were on???

ElNinaOH And me 😌

Ells010 What?? Why did no one tell me?

ElNinaOH It was just a scout – luckeeeeeee 😌

Maya386 You can't compete anyway Ellie

Ells010 So? I can next month

Tamz777 It'll take you months to get your strength back Ellie

Maya386 Coach doesn't reckon you'll be back on the team this year. She's given your space on the Brighton trip to Amy.

Ells010 left the group

'What's all the big deal about?' Onyx asks me, as I stuff my phone away, making sure I've turned it off.

'Coach makes such a big deal about committing to

the squad, but as soon as you get ill or have an injury, she dumps you. It's ruthless. I'm so glad I'm out of it.'

'Sounds rubbish,' Onyx says, idly watching the skateboarders practising ollies.

'Oh, I forgot to tell you yesterday with all the trauma!' I jump up, grabbing her arms.

'Oh, so it's okay for you to manhandle me?' Onyx says in mock upset.

'The auditions. Come and look.'

The list is tacked to a corkboard next to the drama studio. Ms Latimer is in there on the phone. She waves through the glass and carries on talking.

'*The Circus of Dreams*,' Onyx reads.

'You know it?' I ask reading over the names. Barnabas is popular. There is a massive list of names. I spot Ellie's and Maya's and Lara's too.

'*On freedom's side. We can't be denied. On freedom's, freedom's siiide!*' Onyx sings.

'Not you as well.'

'What? I love that song. It's all about acceptance and strength,' Onyx says, making a fist in the air.

'I put our names down for backstage, but do you want to try for a part?' I ask.

'Me? Nah. I like shows, but I don't really want to act.'

'Why do you go to drama club then?'

'Because you do. Because Ms Latimer is nice.'

'Oh, right,' I say, beaming.

'So, who are you putting down for?'

'Me? No. I can't sing.'

'This is why you dragged me over here. Come on. Who?' Onyx demands, pulling me to face her.

'Eee. Owww. Eye contact. Burning,' I say, trying to squirm away from her gaze. 'Oh, okay. I want to do the tightrope-walker one.'

Onyx lets go of me. 'That's better. So, which one is she? Rosemary?'

'Yuck, no. She has to do kisses. No, stop. What are you doing?' I try to grab the pen that Onyx has produced, but it's too late. She writes at the bottom of the list: *Please let Mo try out for the tightrope walker – we don't know her name.*

'Ohhhh, ONYX! That's *sooo* embarrassing.' I cover my face with my hands.

'Don't be daft. It's fine. Come on, the bell's about to go.'

FRIDAY 8 OCTOBER

I've almost forgotten about Denham this week, with the trauma of not having Onyx in my class anymore, and then worrying about the auditions. The times went up yesterday and I've got my audition to be Clara the tightrope walker today, halfway through lunch. I am terrified. To make it even worse, it is Onyx's appointment day – her psycho day she calls it – so she isn't in to help keep me calm.

I trudge over to the drama studio. I couldn't eat any lunch because my anxiety is churning my stomach like a washing machine. When I arrive, there is an audition going on. Paper has been put over the glass so no one can peep through. That is good and bad. Good because no one will be able to see my epic fail, and bad because I can't see who the interrogators are going to be. Obviously, Ms Latimer is there. I'm guessing Mr Kaspar, the music guy, too. I just hope it isn't anyone else.

The handle moves and the door clicks open. One of the exam students steps out and gives me a small smile as they hold the door open. There's no bolting now…

'Mo!' Ms Latimer smiles at me as I try not to pass out. Mr Kaspar is there and two of the senior students who I've not seen before. They look perfect and tidy and together, and I don't think I'll even be able to open my mouth.

'How are you doing?' Mr Kaspar says.

I nod but can't speak.

'You've made an impression on Ms Latimer already in drama club, Mo, so there's nothing to be afraid of.'

I clear my throat and hear the bark sound explode out of me. 'The thing is, I can't really sing so I don't think I'm really suitable. I mean I like the character of Clara and everything but, well, I think it would probably be better if you picked someone else. I'm quite happy actually to … to help backstage and you've got loads of names—'

'Mo. Mo,' Ms Latimer interrupts. She's got off her stool and is pulling a couple of big mats down from the wall. One of the seniors goes to help her. 'Don't worry about speaking right now. And your character doesn't need to sing a song, the chorus can do it. What we do need, though, is someone who is quite flexible. There isn't going to be a real high-wire in the show, but we would like to have a bit of movement from the actor. Can you show us any of your gymnastic floor moves?'

'Safely obviously.' Mr Kaspar laughs gently.

'Oh. Okay. I'm not really dressed for it.' I point to my uniform. They are smiling at me expecting something though. I turn my back on them for a moment and breathe. I push my toe into the mat Ms Latimer laid out on the floor. It reminds me of the floor mats at gymnastics, and suddenly I'm back there. Back in front of the judges where I'm preparing to show them what I can do. It's no different, is it? I've got black leggings on under my skirt, so I slip off my shoes, my skirt and tie and place them to the side. I keep my back to the teachers and the seniors while I do a couple of warm-up stretches. It's been a while since I did this. My body is longer now. Will I be able to do it still? But I've done this so many times. I can almost see a shape in the air that my body will follow and, for the first time since I left gym, my mind is quiet. Waiting.

I do a front flip first. My landing is wobbly, but then I do a second, finding a better sense of balance, then I back flip and pause, finally facing them.

'Brilliant.' One of the seniors smiles.

'And if there is a line on the floor, here,' Ms Latimer lays a ribbon out, 'can you walk across it?'

'Well, I was mainly vault, but I did bar too.' I walk

across the ribbon one way, holding my feet as I was taught, then I turn and do a cartwheel back along it.

'Bravo.' Ms Latimer smiles. 'Now will you just read this out for me?'

I take the paper in my hand. My breathing is steadier now.

'But Mr Barnabas! Mr Barnabas. You promised us. We put our trust in you and this, *this* is how you repay us? You pulled us out of the gutter, for what? To throw us back again? What about Molly-Mae? What about Sid? You expect us to go back? Pretend like this never happened? We can't unknow what you've given us. You've given us hope, Mr Barnabas. Don't take that away.'

'See what I mean?' Ms Latimer says to Mr Kaspar. He mimes holding his fist to his chest and I realise that is the pose I am making.

'Brilliant, Mo. Really brilliant.' He stands up and goes to shake my hand, which feels a bit weird, especially as I'm sweaty from doing gym moves.

'We can't say who will be successful until we've seen everyone but that was heartfelt and powerful. Really.' Ms Latimer smiles at me again.

I nod, grab my stuff and walk out of the door. It isn't until I'm halfway to HWE that I realise I still have my skirt in my hand.

SATURDAY 9 OCTOBER

'You're making me go to a library at the weekend, why?' Onyx complains, as I drag her through the shopping arcade.

'There is a local-history section and I want to look up any references to my great uncle. My mum has his name now. He was Albert David Hughes.'

'And we can shop after?' she grumbles. 'Mum is only giving me two hours with you. Dad's in Glasgow, but I think she's paranoid that he has spies from church watching me.'

'Really? That is messed up. Look, once we've done this, we'll go for an ice cream. Come on!'

'Oh goody!' she jokes, and then skips in front of me.

Onyx is always so much happier when her dad is away and I'm taking her to one of my favourite places. I love Brynffynnon library. The wooden shelves and desks are all polished and shiny, and I love the hush that rises up to the ceiling, like quiet smoke. The historical society has their own room and I've been allowed to visit because I told them I was doing a project for history. I didn't say it has nothing to do with school.

Onyx keeps stopping, lifting books off shelves and giving them a sniff. 'Ooh, try this.' She hands me an old hardback. I look at her confused and take a sniff.

'Best drugs.' She grins at me. 'Old-book-smell high.'

'Shhh!' I whisper, pointing at the people working at the desks. 'Come on.'

The historical society has a whole display area dedicated to *Denham Hospital Through the Ages*. I take out my phone and start collecting some images.

'Look, it opened in 1858.'

'Ew, look!' Onyx points at a display cabinet in the corner which houses a straitjacket. It is old with yellowing straps wrapped around the mannequin's body.

'Woah.'

'When was your great uncle there?'

'Well, we don't know that Albert was in Denham, but Mum reckons he probably was. Her family have lived around Brynffynnon for generations. They used to own a grocery store near the marketplace. Albert was Taid's older brother and Taid was born in 1935. Mum doesn't have any records of Albert's death. He had no children and she thinks he probably died in there. Imagine spending your whole life in a kind of prison.'

My eyes drink in all the old photos on the display. There are newspaper cuttings too, about the new treatments and another about a doctor's retirement. They are from the forties. I scan the faces wondering.

'It wasn't really a prison though. It was a hospital.' Onyx challenges.

'Yeah, one where they strapped you to a bed for hours on end – worse than a prison.'

All the images on display make it look like a nice place to recover, but my research has told me what really went on in these places behind closed doors, when no one was looking.

'What's this then?' Onyx points out an old book in a glass-topped display case.

'Oh wow. That is a records book. I can't read the writing easily though.' My nose touches the glass and my breath makes a steam patch.

'That isn't helping.' Onyx smirks. 'Let me see.' She rubs away my mist and reads. 'That's the name column there.' She points. 'And that is a date column. That one says – mal – malard'

'Maladies – it's an old word for illness.'

'Ooh. Mental disorder. Hysteria. Look! Can you see?'

'What are the dates?'

'On this page – 1919. Oh look "shellshock".'

'And this one.' I point at the column on the far right. 'It says "treatments" and that one says "discharge".'

'Loads of them don't have a discharge date – only a line.'

We both look at each other. Onyx draws a finger across her throat – the sign of doom.

'Oh, it is lovely to see young people taking so much interest in history.' A lady with keys on a chain is standing in the door. 'I'm Margaret. I just came to see if there was anything I could help you with.'

'Yes, please!' I blurt out. 'Can you open this so we can look at the register? I think my great uncle might have been at Denham and I want to look at different dates.'

'Oh yes, okay. I'll have to handle the book itself, but I can turn the pages for you. I'll just get the gloves. One moment and I'll be back.'

'Gloves?' Onyx whispers.

I nod as Margaret returns with white gloves on her hands. She takes her jangle of keys and immediately goes to the correct one, slotting it into the sliver circle and turning. She lifts out the register and places it gently on the glass. 'We're only allowed to have the older register on display. Because of data protection, the register from the seventies might have names of people who are still living. But we're okay with this one. So what dates were you looking for?'

'Well, Taid was born in 1935 and he was a few years younger than Albert. They wouldn't have put him in when he was too little, would they?' I ask.

'A lot of mental health problems would arise when children became teenagers,' Margaret says. 'Or children became too troublesome for parents to handle, and they'd get sent there.'

'Why not try around 1940 then?' Onyx suggests.

Margaret flips through the pages looking for dates that could match.

I glance briefly at Onyx. Some things haven't changed much. I think of all the names we get called between us on a daily basis: freak, weirdo, emo, loser; just because we aren't Maya and Ellie clones. The way that Onyx's dad thinks something is wrong with her because she doesn't fit his idea of a perfect daughter.

'So many names.' I breathe.

'Yes, there were over eight-hundred beds in the 1940s. Oh look here.' The dates begin to show 1940. Margaret turns the register so we can read it too. She pulls up a stool for herself and indicates we can do the same.

'It might take a while.' She smiles.

'Loads died from TB.' Onyx notices.

'What's self-murder?' I ask.

'Suicide.' Margaret explains. 'TB was common

in those days and spread quickly in overcrowded conditions. Suicide was common too, sadly. The mental health treatments were in their infancy and often people suffered terribly.'

I'm not really listening. My finger is tracing the names, without touching the paper, looking for an Albert. We move through the pages gradually.

'Is that him?' Onyx says, but no. Albert Arthur Graham is the wrong name.

We move on to 1941. We are almost at the end of the register, and I can see Margaret checking her watch. Onyx is losing interest too, stepping from foot to foot and twisting her wrist braid.

'Oh wait. Hey – could that be him?' Onyx forgets and stabs the paper with a finger.

'Bertie David Hughes,' I read out loud. 'I'm looking for Albert, not Bertie.' I sigh.

'But Bertie is short for Albert. Maybe that's what he preferred to be called so they put it in the register so the staff would know?' Onyx suggests.

I look at the entry.

Name: Bertie David Hughes

Age: 16 years

Admittance: 13 April 1941

Maladies: mental retardation/schizophrenia?

Treatment: prefrontal leucotomy
Discharge:

I realise I've stopped breathing and deliberately take a deep breath in.

'That could really be him.' I stare up at Onyx, amazed at our success. 'Can I take a photo of the entry for my mum?'

'Of course, then I'm afraid I'm going to have to put this away. Stephen, that's my colleague, will think I've been abducted!' Margaret jokes.

I smile briefly, but concentrate on making sure I get clear shots of the entry. 'Why doesn't it have a date for discharge?' I ask Margaret, as she is putting the register carefully back in the glass cabinet.

'Mmm. They may have forgotten to fill it in – if he was there a long time and they began a new register?' Margaret gently ushers us out in front of her, shutting the historical society's door behind us.

'Maybe he never left,' Onyx says meaningfully.

'Crikey.'

'Come on, Professor, let's go eat ice cream,' Onyx says, pulling at my arm.

So, we say our thank yous and goodbyes and then Onyx is dragging me out of the main door into the weak October sunlight.

'It's crazy to think there were so many people kept in that old building,' I muse, nodding in the direction of Denham.

'So many ghosts!' Onyx laughs.

'We have to find the basement. Bertie had a pre-frontal leucotomy. You know what that was right?'

'No. ICE CREAM.' She makes whirly shapes in front of my face as though she is trying to hypnotise me.

'Lobotomy. They were doing the operations right there! You saw the place,' I say excitedly. 'It was just abandoned. They didn't even bother to clear away little stuff like plates and cups. I bet all the medical equipment is still there! The places where they kept the most difficult patients. I've got to go back, Onyx. I've got to find out what they did to him. Just me and you, okay?'

TUESDAY 12 OCTOBER

'Hey emo,' Ellie says, settling in front of me in form room. She appears to have chosen her own new seat, and the form tutor doesn't seem to have much say in it. Ellie pats her bag tidily with her good hand. I stare balefully at Ellie.

'What? It's only a joke, Mo! Can't you take a joke?'

'Jokes are supposed to be funny.' I remind her.

Instead of a bad comeback she just shuffles in her seat, checking her phone for messages in her bag. I can see there are no new notifications. Maya and the wannabes don't even glance over today, and suddenly I realise how lonely Ellie probably is right now. I remember how I felt that day I quit gymnastics.

'Are you missing training?' I ask.

She nods. 'Yeah, a bit. Dad phoned Coach and my place on the squad *IS* still there but,' she sighs, 'it will take me a while to get my strength back in my arm. It's the cartwheels and handstands. I can go back next week, but I won't be able to do much.'

'You'll get your strength back,' I say.

‘Thanks, Mo.’ She smiles at me briefly.

‘We find out about the auditions today,’ I say.

‘OMG,’ Ellie squeals. ‘Is it really today? I CAN’T wait! I wonder who I’m gonna be!’

‘Shush, Ellie,’ the tutor says, as he starts to mark us in.

Lunchtime takes forever to come. Despite having history, the wait to find out about the auditions drags on the day like a stroppy toddler. When the bell goes at the end of maths, we head over to the drama studio.

‘Hurry up!’ Onyx jumps in front of me. ‘Don’t you want to know?’

‘Honestly, it’s no big deal. I really don’t mind if I get it. In fact, it’s probably going to be a whole load easier for my life if I don’t get it. I mean, can you imagine the stress.’

‘Stop waffling,’ Onyx says, grabbing my arm. ‘You will be amazing. We need to see!’

The list has gone from the noticeboard. Ms Latimer and the seniors are in the studio already and quite a few students are milling about chatting. There are a lot of the older kids here and it is quite a squeeze to find a place to stand. I’m quite happy to wait by the door but Onyx drags me inside, pushing against bags and squeezing past people to find a place.

After a few more moments, Ms Latimer clears her throat, and the room goes quiet.

'Hi everyone. Firstly, we'd like to say thank you to you all…' she pauses here and glances at the seniors who nod, '…for your interest. We're pretty overwhelmed to be honest!'

The door – open as people are wedged in the entrance – is forced open even wider as Mr Kaspar enters. Everyone makes a little path for him to reach Ms Latimer.

'Yes. Sorry I'm late. We really were blown away by the level of ability too,' Mr Kaspar says, pushing his hand through his hair.

'So, if you aren't given a part this year, remember there are plenty more opportunities for you. Most of the larger roles go to exam students,' Ms Latimer explains.

Onyx makes a little sad face at me at this point.

'So, if you are in year seven and year eight don't be put off. You can always come to drama club to improve your skills! But, without further ado, I'm going to read the list of parts and students' names alongside.' Ms Latimer fiddles with her glasses and clears her throat. 'Barnabas – Lara Greenwood.' Ms Latimer pauses for the cheers to subside. 'Rosemary – Lydia Matek.' The senior on the panel smiles as others congratulate her.

'Colin – Ifan Davies.' The boy with the moustache bows, as someone pushes him playfully.

Ms Latimer continues to read out the list of the characters. My stomach is twisting. I really don't know if I want to hear my name or not. I see Ellie at the edge looking more and more disappointed with every name call.

'Clara – Mo Prendergast,' Ms Latimer calls, giving me a beaming smile.

'YeSSSSS!!!' yells Onyx, as she attacks me in a hug. Other people around me are congratulating me and patting my shoulders. A gush of breath comes out – a sort of laugh, a sort of choke. And I feel my legs shaking a little. I've gone and got a part!

Ellie does have a part, she is the daughter, but she still doesn't look massively happy about it. Sambhav is the son. The rest of the year sevens are in the chorus.

'You're the only year seven with a main part, Mo!' Onyx says excitedly. The seniors have handed scripts out and we are skimming over the pages.

'Clara's not really a main part.' I point out.

'She so is! She's in loads of scenes. Look! Not the first two, but then you come in scene three and are pretty much on stage for the rest of the play. Look, act one: scene three is just you!'

'Oh gawd. Really?' I feel flushed and jittery and as though I want to scream with excitement and fear.

'I knew you'd smash it,' Onyx says, giving me a side hug.

I feel like I'm winning at life for the first time.

A lot of people have left the room now, and just those who have acting parts are left. Onyx stays next to me, even though she is only down to help with scenery, but Ms Latimer doesn't make her leave.

'Happy?' Mr Kaspar asks. Everyone nods and grins in response.

'We will be starting rehearsals from tomorrow. They'll be every Wednesday in the hall after school – 3.30 until 5 p.m. Any problems with that, stay behind and let us know. And once again, well done!' Ms Latimer beams at us.

Everyone starts to leave, chatting excitedly as the bell rings for afternoon lessons.

'Well done, little bug.' Lara claps me on the back.

'Thanks. And you! Barnabas is amazing.'

'You didn't fancy acting?' Lara asks Onyx.

Onyx flushes. 'No, err. I'm just helping.'

'That's great too. See you tomorrow, Mo,' Lara calls, as they head off with their friends.

Ellie is still arguing her case with Ms Latimer

that she should be given a better part. 'Daughter? Daughter! Really? With my talents.'

'Carys? Can I have a word?' Ms Latimer calls out, cutting Ellie off entirely. 'This is private, Ellie. I'll see you tomorrow.' Ms Latimer walks towards us. 'You can stay, Mo, it's fine.' She shuts the door and perches on the edge of a desk that is pushed against the wall. 'Mr Pebbles has been to see me,' she says gently to Onyx, 'about your dad's wishes.'

Onyx makes a face.

'For the record I entirely disagree with him. I don't think Mo is a bad influence on anyone and I think that you both being such good friends is lovely.'

I feel like I am filling up with sharp little pieces of gravel. Onyx looks like she might start crying again.

'But, Mr Pebbles is concerned as your dad is threatening to remove you from Ysgol Offa entirely. So in that light, I think he wants to respect your dad's wishes. Which means—'

'He's not going to let me help with the play, is he?' Onyx turns toward the wall and rubs her face.

Ms Latimer shakes her head sadly. 'You can still come to club at lunchtimes though.'

Onyx nods, her eyes filling with tears. I feel like all the gravel has filled me up to the throat, I can't even speak.

'Okay, off to lessons then you two.'

I hug Onyx and head off on my own to my science lesson wondering if there is nothing her dad can't ruin. If only I could be a different person, maybe he wouldn't mind Onyx being my friend? Going to Denham is going to be more important than ever. It's the only place we are ever going to be able to spend any time together.

WEDNESDAY 13 OCTOBER

I thought maths had turned a corner, but things have become even worse. Miss Pool sat me next to Sambhav at the front, so I can see the board, but I'm right under her nose. I just need to breathe and she has a go at me.

Today I'm kept in because I forgot to include my working out. I have to rewrite the whole piece in breaktime.

'Why did you forget to include your working out, Maureen?' Miss Pool stands over my desk after everyone has left.

'I don't know. I was concentrating on getting the an—'

She leans in over me. 'Look at me when I'm speaking to you.'

I bring my gaze up as close as I can to her eyes, focusing on her eyebrows.

'I'll tell you why you forgot. Because you're stupid and you're lazy and you enjoy making my life difficult. If it wasn't for you, I wouldn't have had the deputy head at the back of my class last Monday. Now get it done or it'll be an after school.'

She lets the door slam as she leaves the room with a coffee cup in her hand.

I can't help it. A tear rolls down my nose. I wipe it away quickly with the back of my hand. No adult's ever called me stupid before, or lazy. I can't believe she's just said it. The words echo around my head as I try to remember the steps I went through to get the answers and all the rules she insists on. I'm dying for the toilet and too scared to go.

I was looking forward to today's rehearsal, but when the bell for the end of the day goes, I still feel flat and wrong. I say goodbye to Onyx and head over to the hall. A few people are there already, sitting on chairs that are laid out in rows in front of the stage.

I see some people from my class: Ellie, Sambhav, Harry, Soraya and Chantelle. I wander over and wait with them, not really feeling like saying much.

'OMG, Mo, you got such a good part,' Ellie says. 'Ms Latimer wanted to give Clara to me but because of my arm she thought it best to let you have it.'

'Course she did, Ellie,' I say.

Ellie completely misses my sarcasm. 'Yeah, because of the gymnastic moves. She's gonna write me some extra lines for my part, though.'

'I don't mind being in the chorus,' Chantelle says. 'I love the soundtrack!'

She, Sambhav and Soraya join in with a chorus of *On freedom's side*. Something tells me I'm going to be sick of that song by Christmas.

'Attention, everyone!' calls Ms Latimer from the stage. 'Thank you, thank you. Okay. Shhhh. So, today we will be moving into groups. In a moment, the chorus will be going with Mr Kaspar to learn the songs in the music room. Those of you in the family will be working in the drama studio with Rudi.' Rudi stands up and waves. 'That is Mother, Daughter and Son.' She looks up to check we have all understood. 'And the rest of you: so Barnabas and the troupe, as well as Billy Whizz, you'll be staying in here with me. We will all be back together in two or three weeks, but until then go directly to your area at each rehearsal. Okay?'

The hall thins out as the chorus and family leave, leaving a dozen of us behind. Apart from me, everyone is doing GCSEs and A-levels. I shuffle slightly lower in my seat and my feet start to clench in my shoes. I wish Onyx was here.

'Well then.' Ms Latimer rubs her hands. 'This is where it's all going to happen. We're going to make magic on this stage.' She gestures to where she is standing. 'It's really important that you all get used to being up here, so with the main parts we will practise from day one on stage. I know some of you have performed in the school before, but not all – Charlie hasn't and neither has Mo.'

'I have, but not at this school.' Charlie pipes up.

'Okay. Let's do it. Come on up and bring your scripts!'

There is a scrape of chairs as people make their way to the steps and up onto the wooden stage.

'Come on, Mo.' Lara beckons me to go with them and waits at the foot of the steps so we can go up together. I smile gratefully. On the stage it is a completely different viewpoint. I look down at the rows of empty plastic chairs and to the back of the hall where tall glass windows open to the playing field. When I was doing vault there would be a few dozen parents at the most. When this hall is full, though … how will I cope?

'Make a circle, folks,' Ms Latimer says. I stand between Lara and the senior playing Rosemary. 'We're going to play a warm-up game, okay? It will help you learn names as well as make you feel a bit more relaxed. You have to throw the bean bag at someone while you say your name and "I like…" and here you say a food. The first person has to start with a food beginning with the letter A and then we go in order through the alphabet. So, I say: I'm Ms Latimer and I like apples, I throw it to…' She throws the bean bag to the kid playing Beans and he says:

'I'm Charlie and I like bananas.'

And so we start our rehearsal. By the time the bean bag gets to me we're on G, so I like 'grapes' and throw it to Sal. After that we do some reading from act one: scene three, which is when Barnabas starts recruiting us all for his circus. It's fun in the end and does take my mind off maths and Onyx's stupid dad.

THURSDAY 14 OCTOBER

I'm dreading maths. The rocks are back in my stomach.

'Dad, I don't feel well,' I say, sitting on the stairs as he brushes his teeth.

'Uh?' he says, as he spits in the sink. 'What's up?'

'I think its period pains,' I lie. I finished my period just over a week ago and even I know they come every month, not every week.

'Oh, MoMo,' Dad says, coming out and ruffling my hair. 'Diane? What can Mo do about period pains?'

She's in the bedroom changing Stink's nappy. 'Paracetamol,' she calls back.

'Okay. Paracetamol and you should be okay.'

'Do I have to go in?' It isn't too late to leave home for my fantasy den in the woods. Even with the autumn weather. It has to be better than school.

'I don't think you can stay off for period pains, MoMo. Come on, let's go find a tablet.'

The day drags slower and slower as we get closer to maths. We all line up outside Miss Pool's room waiting for the command to enter, but it doesn't come.

People start chatting and Mylo starts pushing people about, until a tall thin man with a goatee walks into Miss Pool's room.

'Supply.' Harry grins gleefully.

'Sit where we want.' Soraya fist bumps Chantelle.

Relief scours my insides. Nothing can be worse than Miss Pool.

At breaktime, Onyx and I are huddled together on the wall under her umbrella.

'Mo's been. Haven't you, Mo?' a voice shouts.

Onyx raises the umbrella so we can see who's calling me. The football crowd have come into the yard because the weather is bad and Sambhav is doing keepie-uppies, trying to avoid the puddles.

'Where have I been?'

'To the lunatic asylum – Denham.' He drops the ball and it lands in a puddle.

'Oh right.' I nod.

'I've just dared Mylo to go,' Sambhav says, coming to stand with us.

'You're not coming with us,' I say crossly. 'We're going back to do a historical investigation.'

'At midnight,' Onyx says. 'On Halloween.'

'What?' I nudge her. 'No, we're not.'

'Seriously?' Mylo says.

'Bet you don't,' Sambhav says. 'Or are you going to do your ouija thing? You know.' He points to the necklace of a pentacle that Onyx is wearing over her jumper.

Some of the boys start laughing.

'Oh, like a witch thing!' Mylo grins.

'Just because I've got this necklace doesn't mean I'm a witch, idiot,' Onyx says.

Mylo has got the ball now and kicks it over into the skaters. Sambhav wanders off to try and retrieve his ball from Lara who is holding it way above their heads.

'I told you we can't go at night; I won't be able to see. And why Halloween?'

'Ah come on, Mo. It'll be more of an adventure,' Onyx says more quietly.

'We just won't be able to see anything. What's the point?'

'You're scared!'

'What of?'

'Ghosts. OoooOooh!' She does a very bad impression of a ghost holding an umbrella.

'Don't be daft. Ghosts don't exist.'

'Well, if they don't exist there's no reason not to go at night, is there? There is no way I'm going to escape in the day for long enough to go to Denham anyway,' she says, bitterly. 'Remember, I live in a prison. I've worked it all out. I'm going to go to bed as usual, and then sneak out when they're both in the lounge. The back-door key's always on a hook in the kitchen. They'll never know I'm gone. We won't have to rush and can explore the whole place. Come on. You know there's nothing to be afraid of, so why not?'

'How will we see?' I ask, realising that going at night may be our only way to get to see each other outside of school breaktimes.

'We've got some good torches, that'll last for ages. I can borrow them, they won't notice.'

I stare at her. 'Is this the only way we can do this?'

'Yes! I want to do something different, something wild. It'll make it more exciting.' Onyx's eyes look glittery.

I get what she's saying about having more time, and it is true that her folks won't let her out of their sight. Even her mum gets jittery if we want to meet up now.

Mr Pebbles is walking across the yard. I think he has come to tell the kids off for playing footy here – they aren't supposed to. But he is walking toward us.

I shrug. 'Okay if we have to. But only because you're my friend.'

Onyx grins wide and hugs me tight.

'Carys, Mo,' Mr Pebbles nods at us both. 'I'm sorry, girls, but you know you aren't allowed to mix at school. Mr Melling does not want Carys to be spending time with you, Mo. You are going to have to find somewhere else to spend your breaks.' And without any discussion, he ushers us off in different directions.

FRIDAY 15 OCTOBER

When I told Dad about Onyx not being in my class anymore and not being allowed to spend time with me, he said a swear word and Diane shouted at him. It would be funny if Stink's second word was the 'B' word.

It feels like the worst kind of torture. Finally, I find someone who likes me, and I'm banned from seeing them. Friday is family film night so we are all going to crash on the sofa and watch a spooky film. Hopefully it will take my mind off school and Onyx.

'Ewan's asleep, so keep the noise down, you pair.' Diane closes the door gently behind her and pads into the lounge.

That's her line whenever she's been putting Stink to bed. She looks cross, but Dad has a bottle of wine in his hand and her face relaxes.

'Not another horror film, please!' she says, as she collects a couple of glasses from the sideboard.

'Yes, another horror film!' I say.

We have to watch Halloween films. It's not far

off Halloween now and I like watching them. Mum won't let me watch them in case I have nightmares. But seriously, they are hilarious. Me and Dad know the formula – flickering lights, spooky music, usually someone levitating, doors slamming on their own. Dad says we could make millions writing them ourselves.

'What about this one?' Dad says pausing over the image of a film called *Demoneyes*.

'Read out the blurb,' Diane asks. 'I haven't got my glasses.'

'When emo kid, Harley, moves to a new part of town, the family's dream house has more to it than it first appears. She finds a ouija board in her basement and all hell's unleashed…'

'It sounds like the usual rubbish.' Diane laughs, but seems happy enough to go along with it. She must have had a good day with Stink because she is in a relaxed mood. She's even got us the biggest tub of popcorn this week.

'What does emo mean anyway?' I ask, as I take the popcorn tub she hands me.

'Emo is like, sort of goth, I think?'

'I was a bit emo in my time. My Chemical Romance.' Dad smiles wistfully.

'Always feeling depressed and miserable, I imagine.' Diane laughs. 'You know *emo*tional.'

'No! That's a generalisation. I think it's more about music and style. Look at the kid on the pic.' Dad points at the film image of where the main character is looking terrified, with their black fringe across their eyes and a crucifix earring glowing red. Onyx has the black fringe, I guess, but that's where the similarity ends.

'None the wiser,' I say, grabbing a handful of popcorn out of the tub.

'Black clothes mainly, cool hair.' Dad points to his receding hair line.

'Just put it on then,' Diane says, shaking her head. 'Anything to make you be quiet for a minute.'

'Rude,' says Dad. He shifts onto the armchair to squash next to me, pressing play at the same time.

After the film, I go to my room. My room at Dad's house is smaller than at Mum's. I like the bed best, as the mattress is so comfy.

I'm not ready for sleep even after a drag of my blanket, so I pull my script out of my bag and begin to read through the words:

Barnabas and the Circus of Dreams

A play for schools in two acts

...is written on the front. Inside is a list of characters and then the first scene. The first bit is at Barnabas' house before he starts the circus, so I'm not in that. My first scene is scene three. After that I'm in a lot of scenes, like Onyx said, but luckily I don't have to say loads. I say a couple of lines in the fight at the end of act one, but my main bit is in act two.

My stomach feels churny as I think of rehearsing and standing on the stage to speak. I've no idea if I'll be able to do it. I wish Onyx was doing the acting too. She makes me feel braver. I've never really understood what it means to be friends, and now I've finally got one her dad is trying to destroy it.

I fall asleep dreaming of being on the stage, but the stage is in Denham. The only audience is George, Onyx's dad, and Miss Pool. Ivy curls tight around my ankles and when I begin to say my lines, instead of words coming out of my mouth, broken teeth spit across the audience like miniature missiles.

MONDAY 18 OCTOBER

Ten more school sleeps to half term! I'm not counting weekends because it makes it sound longer. I'm seeing Mum later too, which makes getting into school this morning a tiny bit more bearable. Maths though. Maths makes me feel like a small whale is lodged in my stomach. Not good.

Onyx and I aren't supposed to meet at break anymore, but before the school bell goes there are no teachers on duty. I give Onyx a hug. She's been doodling and has drawn a tree with bare branches and a moon behind it.

'That's good,' I say, as I sit down next to her.

'Mmm.' She shrugs her shoulders and barely looks up.

'Do you like My Chemical Romance?' I ask her as I watch Sambhav and a couple of his friends saunter across with the ball.

'What is that?' She looks up at me then, peeking through her fringe as usual.

'Oh, just some ancient band my dad used to like.'

'My dad just listens to classical music, apart from at Christmas when he pushes the festive boat out and puts Cliff Richard on.' She makes the vomit gesture.

'Cliff Richard? It really IS bad at your house, isn't it?' I say.

'You've no idea, Mo.'

When Mum picks me up at the end of the day, I want to hug her and never let go. It's been a long few days without her.

'Hey, is everything okay?' After a long hug, she holds my face and scans over it. 'What's up, Mo?'

I want to tell her about Onyx and her dad; about Miss Pool and how she treats me, about how I dread her classes; about Denham. But I don't know how to start the conversation. All the awfulness of it is lodged in my throat, like an ugly pineapple.

'I just feel I haven't seen you for about a month.'

'We can have a good catch up today.' She eases the car into gear and into the stream of traffic. 'It's brilliant news about the play.'

'Yeah.' I lean my head back against the seat and close my eyes. My hand reaches into my bag to feel for blanket. Being with Mum is the best. I love Dad. Even Stink. Diane's okay. But being with Mum is like after swimming when you just feel like every muscle is relaxed.

'Dad said you had period pains again. It sometimes takes a while for your cycle to settle when you first start.'

'I just didn't want to go to school. I didn't really have any pain.' I confess, half opening my eyes to catch her expression.

'Oh MoMo,' she tuts, but gently. 'Any particular reason?'

'Maths. I hate maths.' But that's all she gets, because I pretend I've fallen asleep and just enjoy the jolt of the car as we travel around the corners and turn towards home.

TUESDAY 19 OCTOBER

Ellie is perched at the edge of our wall watching the boys playing football.

'I think she's lonely.' I shrug.

'Well, she deserves to be. She's a total bitchington!' Onyx mutters.

We are both watching the teacher who is on duty, knowing any minute now they are going to walk over and tell us to separate.

I watch Ellie pointlessly taking out her hairbrush and running it through her immaculate hair.

'You should tell her to leave us alone,' Onyx continues, whispering to me. 'She's always been so nasty to you and me, and then just thinks she can hang around us!'

'Yeah,' I agree, but I know I won't say anything to Ellie. I find it all too difficult to put into words. Onyx is right, Ellie has been awful to both of us, but … I just remember gymnastics and how intense it all was. It's hard not having friends. I don't know what I'd do without Onyx, even though her dad is trying to keep us apart.

The duty teacher gestures to us to go elsewhere, as though she is brushing away dust in separate directions.

Onyx scowls at her and stalks away from me.

At the end of the day, when I reach Mum's car, she is deep in conversation with Ellie's mum. I nod at them without speaking and clamber into the front seat, shutting the door on all the noise of kids shouting and cars revving. A moment later, Mum gets in, still saying goodbyes as she slams the door shut.

'That woman!' Mum hugs me briefly and starts the car up. 'She hasn't spoken to me since you quit gymnastics, and now I can't shut her up!'

'What was she saying?'

'Oh, she was complaining about Coach, about the other girls – they're leaving Ellie out apparently. Do you fancy a hot chocolate? I've got to pick a couple of bits up from the shop?'

'Can I have cake?'

'Whatever you want.' She smiles.

Luckily the cafe is quiet when we go in and order. I lick the top of my drink where chocolate dusting patterns the cream.

'Don't let me forget parents' evening tomorrow,'

Mum says, as she scrolls through the calendar on her phone.

'Is Dad coming too?'

'Should be. Is there anything you want me to ask, or any subject you're struggling with? You don't talk to me much about school anymore, MoMo.' Mum touches my hand.

I shrug as I stir the creamy layer into the deep brown with the long spoon. I could tell her about maths, but my mouth won't make the words. The churning sick feeling rises up as I think of it.

'Hmm. Well, it will be good to see your different teachers anyway. They can tell me how you are doing, can't they?' Mum is giving me her laser gaze.

I can't look at her; my eyes will tell her how maths is the Toilet of Doom.

'I'll message your dad now to remind him, just in case.' She fiddles with her phone again.

'You're always telling me not to spend too much time on my phone.'

'Yes. True. Sorry.' She slips it in her pocket. 'So, Ellie's mum was making out you and Ellie are best friends.'

'No!' I snort my hot chocolate, dripping some on the table. 'I hang around with Onyx.'

'That's what I thought.'

'But I do feel sorry for Ellie. She was mean to me, and Onyx thinks I shouldn't talk to her. But I feel like I could cry thinking about her not being able to do acro.'

Mum sighs and puts her coffee cup down. 'Ah, hyper-empathy,' she says.

'Mum!' I moan. Nev jokes about how Mum likes a label for *everything*. 'In normal language?' I sip my drink and feel the gloopy warm sweetness in my mouth.

'It's just some of us autistics, well I guess just some people, it doesn't have to be autistics, but it is more common in auti—'

'MUM!' I say louder than I mean. 'Hyper-empathy?'

'Oh well. It's when you feel the other person's feelings so much, they sort of swamp your own. You feel like you are drowning in them.' She forces herself to stop and smiles at me.

'Oh.'

'It can be useful. You just have to be careful not to lose sight of your feelings and yourself.'

'I am full of love and desire for this piece of carrot cake right now,' I say, as I dip the fork into the creamy icing.

'Yes, when feeling overwhelmed, focus on cake.' She grins as I cram in the biggest mouthful and start to chew.

WEDNESDAY 20 OCTOBER

We are rehearsing in the drama studio not the hall today, as they are setting up for parents' evening. I'm going to meet Mum and Dad as soon as I've finished the rehearsal.

There are only the circus performers today. We are in a circle with Ms Latimer in the middle in full swing.

'To help you all get into character, it's important you understand why your character is in the situation they are in,' Ms Latimer says. 'Every character has some kind of difference, that in Victorian times would have been seen as a negative or bad thing. So, for example, Mia is albino.' She nods toward a tall girl in the circle. 'And Sid is mute. Talk to the person next to you about what your character's difference is and how it might make them feel in a world that isn't accepting. Two minutes.'

I hope to catch Lara's eye, but they're talking to Ms Latimer. Tyler, who plays Billy Whizz looks at me and turns her back, clearly not wanting to be partnered with the year seven. Charlie, the new kid from year ten, turns to me and grins.

'Hey, you're Mo, right?'

I nod. I am not sure I am even going to be able to speak, I feel so nervous.

'Well, I'm Charlie and I'm playing Beans. So, I know that he is a dwarf. Well, I am short for my age, so I know a bit how that feels! Everyone in my year is obsessed with being tall and they kind of look down on me a bit, ha, well, literally, I guess. I kind of feel invisible sometimes. Though I don't let people ignore me because my personality is too big for that!'

He holds his hands out either side of him and raises his eyebrows. It's a gesture I'm not used to, and I don't really know what it means. His face still looks smiley so I'm taking it that it's a positive thing for him. I smile and hope he carries on talking. It means I don't have to.

'I guess in those days it would've been even worse, wouldn't it?' he says. 'I reckon people probably thought people with dwarfism were dumb as well. What about you? Your character's the typical bearded lady of the freak show, right?'

I'm amazed how one person can say so much just like that. There is an embarrassing pause while he waits for me to say something. I nod at him.

'So, how do you think that would feel?'

'Mmm. I'm not sure. Hairy?' I eventually come out with and then I start laughing. Hairy. Really? 'I know about what it feels like to be different, but I've no idea how it would feel to have a beard!' I blurt.

'Hmm.' Charlie is looking serious and not seeing the funny side at all. 'I guess people would have thought you were like an animal?'

Ms Latimer, who's been listening in to the different conversations, reaches us. 'Hi Charlie, Mo. I think you're right. It would've been incredibly hard to live anything like a normal life. People would've made massive assumptions about someone with so much facial hair. Even now women with facial hair are judged harshly.'

I'm desperate to laugh again, but I'm trying to hold it in. The phrase *facial hair* is just feeding into my embarrassment.

'Back then people would have seen only the hair, wouldn't they? They would have imagined some kind of monster, not a human being with feelings,' says Ms Latimer.

'That's why Clara is hiding away when Barnabas comes calling,' Charlie says.

'Yes, she's so used to being treated like a freak and hiding away from the world, but yet she's got this natural agility that Barnabas has heard about.'

'I suppose even the laws and things wouldn't have stopped people being mean,' I say.

'Yes, there was no one to complain to, and no one who would listen,' Ms Latimer says. 'Not like now. Nowadays people aren't allowed to treat others with disrespect because of their difference.' Her gaze lingers on me a little bit too long, so that I feel uncomfortable. It is as though she's about to say something else, but then her facial expression changes once again. 'Okay, folks. Let's rehearse! Scripts at the ready.'

We run through my scene today, and I find that as soon as I start reading my part my worry evaporates. It is almost like being someone else. All the words are on the page, so I know exactly what to say and to do. I think I'm going to really like my character even though I have to wear a beard!

When Ms Latimer says we have to finish off as she has to go and speak to the parents, I feel disappointed. No one else is in year seven so they don't have to go, but I head over to the hall. It has already started and as I search for Mum and Dad, I finally find them just getting up from talking to Miss Pool. My stomach drops like a depressed parrot.

'Your maths teacher is a bit of a battle-axe isn't she?' Dad says as we head home.

I'm looking at the pictures of Denham again on my phone. There are hardly any of the basement, but there is one photo I keep coming back to. There is no window. The camera flash illuminates part of a rusted bed frame. A tall metal object lurks in the shadows, wires dangling from it like exposed veins.

'Miss Pool, Mo, she's a bit of a battle-axe,' Dad repeats.

'A battle-axe?' I ask, finally looking up.

'It means sort of intimidating. Scary.'

I don't reply, just return to my phone.

'Does she help you? She says you're—' he breaks off, '—struggling a bit.'

'I hate her,' I say but, despite him asking me a zillion times, I don't say why.

MONDAY 25 OCTOBER

Miss Pool has stuck me outside maths again for 'fidgeting and distracting others'. It didn't take her long to find an excuse to get me out of her way. I'm trying and failing to work out fractions without any help when Mrs Flax, the headteacher, strides up the corridor. I've only ever seen her from a distance and she's never spoken to me.

She is small and slim and upright and terrifying.

I put my head down and look at the fractions in front of me. I hear her steps coming closer. She pauses every now and then and, risking a glance, I see her peering through the glass window in each classroom door as she gets closer and closer.

I feel her reach me and stop, angled above me like an interrogation lamp.

'Why are you outside?' she asks.

I don't know how to reply. I always sit outside now and all the reasons jumble together stealing my words. I just keep looking at the sum on my page: $6/18 + 5/9 = ?$

She's still waiting for a reply.

'How long have you been sitting out here?' she asks, still poised above me, perfectly still.

'All lesson … I think.' My voice sounds rough and scratchy.

'Get your things,' she says.

I've heard of people having to go to the head's office. Often, it's before they get excluded for something. I wouldn't mind never having to come to school. If it wasn't for the play. And for Onyx.

But she isn't dragging me back to her office, she is opening the classroom door and beckoning me back inside. Miss Pool's face looks funny as her scowls at the sight of me are chased away when she realises Mrs Flax is standing right behind me.

'May I have a word, Miss Pool,' the head says. No one dares speak as I make my way to my seat.

When Miss Pool returns, she seems just the same, apart from a high red splotch on each cheek, as though she has pressed her thumbs against her face. She doesn't speak to me for the rest of the lesson.

FRIDAY 29 OCTOBER

It's drama club today and, as it is the end of the half term, we are allowed to mess about with some Halloween costumes. I'm wearing a werewolf mask and Onyx has a vampire cloak on. We are supposed to be thinking about creating a jump-scare scene, but I can't concentrate.

'Remind me how I am going to get out on Sunday again?' I have been worrying about this for days. My dad's house isn't big like Onyx's house and they are both still up in the night with Stink sometimes.

'So,' Onyx clasps my hands in hers excitedly, 'you are going to say you don't feel well.'

'When the film's on—'

'Yes, then go up to bed and pretend to go to sleep. When you hear them go to bed, you creep downstairs and go out the back door. Key's always in the lock, right?'

'Yes, but what if this is the one night that it isn't? And the back gate really creaks, and their bedroom is at the back; what if Dad or Diane look out and see me? I'll be in so much trouble. Can't I just te—'

'No! They will never let you go if you tell them. It will all be fine. Don't worry!'

'Why is Miss Pool here?' I say dropping my hands to my sides.

Onyx turns to see Miss Pool in the doorway. She is having an animated discussion with Ms Latimer, who beckons Onyx toward her. I follow a step or two behind, suddenly drenched in a feeling of wrongdoing.

'Sorry, Onyx.' Ms Latimer sighs. 'Miss Pool has kindly reminded me that you are not allowed to mix with Mo. I'm afraid you will have to leave club.'

Miss Pool nods her head slightly. She watches as Onyx picks up her bag and coat and slinks out of the studio.

I pull the werewolf mask off my head and slump against the wall. How will we arrange to meet now? Will Onyx even be able to get her phone or the torches? We said the park entrance, but what if I've remembered it wrong? And if her dad finds out, he will have her out of Ysgol Offa before we go back to school. I will never see her again.

SUNDAY 31 OCTOBER

I rub my stomach and groan. 'I've got stomach ache.'

'Probably too many Halloween sweets,' says Dad, not taking his eyes off the screen. He insisted we watch *Ghostbusters* and the marshmallow man is just stomping on New York.

'I think I'm going to head to bed, Dad,' I say, yawning.

Diane looks at me from where she is flopped next to Dad on the sofa. 'You want a drink or anything?'

'I'll get one, it's okay. Night.'

I scurry upstairs. Stink is already in bed, so I'm hoping once the film's finished, they will come straight to bed. He was awake last night and I know Diane is shattered.

After brushing my teeth, I check my bag – sweets, phone, hat and gloves. Then I lie in bed with the duvet over me, heart booming, counting the moments until I *finally* hear the creak of the stairs, the flush of the loo and the thud of their bedroom door shutting. Seconds, then minutes of silence. I wait until finally

I dare to clamber out of bed, stuffing some soft toys and a pillow under the duvet to make a me shape, like they do in the movies.

Opening the door to my bedroom, it floofs slightly on the carpet. Pause. Heart boinging. No sign of stirring from their room, so I tiptoe down the stairs. It is quite a new house so not creaky like Mum's is. I reach the hall downstairs and take a breath. Then I tiptoe through the kitchen, turn the gleaming key in the lock and slowly push the handle down. As I open the back door, sounds from outside filter in, seeming loud as fireworks: a dog barking, a car, someone in the house opposite is talking outside. I shut it behind me quickly, locking and pocketing the key. Then I slide out of the back yard like a bad shadow, through the creaky gate and I run to the park without stopping.

It isn't far from Dad's, only about five minutes through the estate. The air is cold, but not freezing. I've got two hoodies on and gloves in my pocket, as well as my coat. I've never been out this late on my own. The lights from the houses look warm and friendly. The dark places between them do not.

I check my phone. It is already 10.30 p.m. There have been no messages from Onyx at all. What if she doesn't turn up?

There aren't many people about. I see a couple

walking dogs, and some teenagers pass me on the other side of the road. My heart is still playing heavy metal blast beats against my ribs, made worse because I am running and out of breath.

I run out of the estate onto the main road that loops the park. The cars are whizzing by and I wait two or three minutes before a gap in the traffic lets me cross. I see a phone light by the park entrance. Is it Onyx? It glows in the shadows by the railings and I jog the last few metres until I see it is her. It is Onyx!

'Aaaaaahhhh!' is all I can say, as we hug each other and jump up and down.

'All okay?' she asks me.

I nod, still catching my breath and letting my heart rate return to normal.

'This is sooo exciting! My dad would go mental if he knew. He'd lock me up and throw away the key.' Onyx grins.

'It's not funny,' I say miserably. 'I miss you.'

'I miss you too,' she says. She tucks her arm through mine as we begin to walk.

I laugh then. What we're doing feels so grown up and dangerous and exciting all at the same time. We are going to have ages to explore properly and be together without anybody trying to keep us apart. I know we'll find the cages and the medical rooms.

We're going to see it all: the places where my Great Uncle Bertie spent his days; where all those hundreds of other poor people were imprisoned. People like me, my mum, even Onyx. All of us weirdos hidden away from view.

'I hope there are no weirdos about.' I look behind me, to check we aren't being followed.

'Nah. They're all safely tucked up in bed on Halloween,' Onyx replies, grinning at me, 'apart from us two.'

I laugh. 'I don't mean "weird" like us, I mean "weird" like—' I lift my arms out to the side and make a zombie face to show the difference between us and the scary people I was worrying about.

'I don't think you get them in Wales,' she jokes, squeezing my arm.

It's quicker this time because we know the way. The asylum towers above us, its dark shadow pitted with even blacker hollows where windows used to be.

The lights from the town mean we don't even need to put the torches on until we are clambering over the debris at the back of the building. I keep pausing to listen and look behind us.

'No one's there, Mo. Relax!' Onyx says, handing me a chunky torch. 'They're all charged up so should last us for hours. I thought the game was up earlier.

My mum was talking about us going over to visit my aunt, but I begged her to go tomorrow instead and she agreed.'

We pick our way to the window and pull up the metal grill. It is looser than last time, hanging from one corner.

'Someone else has been this way since we last came,' I say.

'Probably Mylo.' Onyx sniggers. 'Let's get a pic.' She fumbles with her phone, holding it up to take a selfie of us both beside the damaged grill.

We look inside. The yawning dark of the room is giving nothing away this evening. It is pitch black. I take my torch and flash it inside. A sudden rush of air and wings makes me squeal and I fall backwards onto the broken slates.

'It was just a pigeon!' Onyx holds her hand out to help me up. 'Your light must've disturbed it.'

We peer inside again, feeling the stale air wafting about us.

'Is this really a good idea?' I look at her face, her eyes glinting in the light.

'Probably not,' she says, scrambling onto the window ledge, 'but it's a fun one.'

We make our way past the manky cupboards and the broken toilet to the first set of stairs. I don't know whether it is the situation or the long night ahead that makes me ask, but it just seems right, so I come out with it, 'Why did you want to call yourself Onyx?'

'I hate my name. It's so girly. It's never fitted me. I've never been interested in the stuff the other girls were into at my old school. That's one reason I left. They were all there with their My Little Ponies and dolls, and then it was painting nails and doing make-up. It wasn't my thing.'

'But you like make-up,' I say, pointing out that she is wearing eyeliner now and eyeshadow.

'My style isn't exactly the same though, is it? Can you imagine Ellie wearing her make-up like this?'

I look at her white make-up and black shading round her eyes. 'I never did those things either. It doesn't matter.'

'I don't think it matters, but my dad did. He thought there was something wrong with me.'

We reach the main entrance. Everything is still and cold. A firework goes off outside and we can just make out the sprinkle of coloured light through a hole in the roof.

'Let's go this way this time,' I say, nodding to a passage across the entrance hall.

'You think?' Onyx says, pausing by the debris. It is the passage we noticed last time we visited, with chunks of fallen roof blocking the way.

'Well, I was never able to find plans of the building, but I've seen enough pictures to have a rough idea of where to look. I'm sure this leads to the basement.'

Onyx clambers over the rubble, getting white powdery dust over her trousers. 'Come on then.' She holds a hand out to me.

'So, that's why you left?' I ask, grabbing her hand as we navigate the uneven floor.

'It's complicated,' Onyx says to me.

'That's okay. I like complicated,' I say.

'The thing is Mo. I'm not a girl.' She pauses and glances at me through her fringe. 'I never have been. My outside body might look like a girl's, but I'm not. It didn't matter when I was little. I was just me and no one minded, but as I get older there's all this expectation to be a certain way. My mum doesn't mind, she just loves me. But my dad – he's made such a big deal out of it.'

'Crikey. He's not doing conversion therapy on you, is he? I read about that when I was doing my research, how they used to think they could make people change, but all it did was make them depressed. It stills goes on in some places.'

'It's a bit like that. That's what these sessions are every week. To try to get to the bottom of why I want to transition. Like he can fix me.'

'What does it mean, to transition?' I scramble over another lump of debris.

'It means I'd be able to dress how I want and define my own gender to start with. Not pretend to be someone I'm not. When I'm older there are other medical treatments too. I could be who I feel I really am on the outside as well as the inside. But my dad would never allow that.'

'I don't see that it is up to him.'

'Neither do I. When I'm old enough I'll leave home and never see him again.'

I'm silent for a few moments trying to process what's been said. We flash our torches up and down the long corridor. There are so many doors off it. Debris crosses our path: old bits of panelling and wire. We peek in the first door on the right. It opens out into a tall room. There are old bedsteads in here. Someone's sprayed pentacles on the wall, and there are empty glass bottles on the floor. Onyx kicks one with her foot, it has a vodka label on it.

'Look,' I say, pointing with the toe of my trainer at an empty hypodermic needle. 'Watch where you step.'

'Druggies.' Onyx makes a face.

We retreat from that room and continue along, looking in every room as we go. There is more of the same, shadows and silhouettes, old broken beds, a wrecked wheelchair, dirt and decay.

As we reach the far end of the corridor, the roof begins to lean down toward the floor, with great wooden slats poking down like broken bones. There is also a set of double doors with an 'Authorised Personnel' sign on them. Onyx pushes them. One is stuck, but the second one does shift enough for us to peer inside. The torchlight picks out a gaping emptiness, and wide steps leading down into blackness.

'This is it!' I grab Onyx excitedly. 'The basement.'

I haven't felt scared until now, but there is something about the absolute blackness, the way the stairs lead into nothing, that makes me want to turn around and run all the way home. I don't believe in spirits, but the names in the register float into my memory, and I can almost imagine them down there, waiting for us.

'I'm not sure that's safe,' I say, suddenly unsure.

'What've we got to lose?' Onyx says. Her face is lit dimly from the torch and her grin has gone. 'Come on.'

She pushes through the door and begins to tread carefully down into the stairwell, her little pool of light bobbing away with her. I sigh and, leaning against the door with my shoulder, follow her down.

We reach the bottom of the stairwell and pause. I'm listening to every sound. There is nothing but a sort of pressing, frozen silence. I reach out for Onyx's hand and she lets me hold it. There are three more sets of double doors leading off. They all have glass in them that reflects the shock of white torchlight back to us. Our shapes wobble and flicker, as though there are things moving beyond.

'This one first?' She moves toward the left-hand doors and pushes them.

'CREAAKKKK.' The noise punches the silence and leaves my heart fighting to escape through my throat. Onyx launches herself through the space into the darkness.

'Woah, Mo. Look.'

In the light of her torch, medical equipment litters the room. There is a giant chair, the leather and stuffing gnawed away, the metal brown with rust. There is a bed on its side and a long tube dangling down from a box attached to the ceiling. There is a cabinet too.

I forget my fear and take my torch over to peer inside the cabinet. It is mainly empty, but there are a couple of broken glass vials on their side, as though dropped moments ago by a doctor too busy to clear them up.

'Take a pic,' Onyx calls. She is sitting on the broken chair, her head dropping to one side in a gruesome way.

'Okay.' I fiddle with my phone. I missed a call from Mum earlier, but it's too late for me to call her back now. I take a pic then stand next to the rusting dirty bed and make a crazy face. 'Take one of me.'

Once we've explored this room, we move to the next double set of doors. The cages must be in here. The cages and the straitjackets…

But no. More of the same: a bed, a decaying chair, a basin in the corner.

THUMP!

I flash the torchlight at Onyx who has paused like a frightened rabbit and is staring at the ceiling.

THUMP! THUMP! THUMP!

I tiptoe over to her as quietly as I can, hardly daring to breathe and turn my torch off.

'What the hell?' I whisper.

'Shush,' she mouths with her finger against her lips, clicking off her torch too and plunging us into blackness.

I listen with every cell in my body. I know what I heard was no ghostly creature, but a living breathing one.

Suddenly loud laughter invades the space, filtering down from above. There is the sound of something dropping. More laughter and footsteps running.

Onyx clings on to me. I can feel her trembling through my coat. I beckon her to come to the wall behind the door. If anyone comes in, we should be able to escape before they see us.

We listen some more. Then more steps, heavier and more steady, above our heads. Voices talking. It seems to go on for ages.

Then the music starts. A heavy repetitive bass track. I hear Onyx sigh next to me.

'The good thing is, they can't hear us now,' I whisper.

'The bad thing is, we're stuck down here,' Onyx replies.

'Yes, but the good thing is, it doesn't sound like they're interested in the basement,' I say.

'Yes, but the bad thing is we're stuck down here,' Onyx groans.

I use my phone light to check there is nothing disgusting on the floor and I lower myself to sit on my haunches. After a moment or two, Onyx does the same.

'Sourstick?' I whisper. I carefully reach inside my bag, take out the snacks and pass her them.

'Thanks!' Onyx slowly tears the packet open, pauses then stuffs a sourstick in her mouth, sucking her cheeks in.

I take a sourstick and suck, feeling the bitterness prickle up the roof of my mouth and make my eyes water. 'At least we've got food,' I murmur.

'Yep. We have food and each other. It'll be okay.' She attempts a small smile.

And that is how we spend the next few hours.

MONDAY 1 NOVEMBER

2 A.M.

Finally, the music stops. We can still hear voices though. They seem louder and more shouty. Someone throws something. There is the sound of smashing glass and stamping feet. I hear swearing and then all goes quiet.

All the excitement of the asylum has gone. I'll be happy if I never see another piece of rusty old medical equipment and I look forward to when the council tears this stupid lump of rubble down and builds some identical semi-detached houses in its place.

I'm not sure if Onyx is still awake. Her head is resting on mine and her breathing seems steady and regular. I leave it a whole half hour without hearing a sound, and I nudge her gently.

'Wake up.'

'Mmm? I wasn't asleep.'

'I think they've gone.'

'Yeah, that's what I thought. Shall we go?'

I stand up and offer my hand to Onyx, helping her up. I use my phone to give us a little light, without the garish shock of the torch. We gently push on the door, trying to avoid the grate and creak of old hinges. Then we creep up the stairs and scurry along the corridor toward the exit. There is the debris from the strange guests littered along the corridor and into one of the rooms – broken bottles, syringes, a T-shirt.

I just want to get out now. I don't care how much Dad will shout at me. I just want to feel safe.

We are just at the bottom of the great staircase when we hear…

'Hey!'

Whoever it is, their footsteps are loud, making the broken tiles crack and the wood splinter.

The noise is coming from our escape route. Without thinking, I run up the big staircase where the night sky glints in at us from above.

'Come on! We can hide,' I call to Onyx.

She races up behind me and we turn in a different direction to the one we explored last time we visited – the time in the daylight, when we could see where we were going.

Heavy footsteps are banging up the stairs behind us. I daren't put my torch on, but keep the light of my phone on our path.

'Oi!' they shout, as we run along the corridor where tendrils of ivy dangle against our skin.

'What do they want?' I breathe, as I try to keep up with Onyx.

'Whatever it is, it's not going to be good, is it? We need to find another way out.' Onyx runs ahead, switching on her torch.

The starlight makes smudges of glitter through the damaged roof. The windows are so grimed up, no light filters through.

This corridor ends in a set of stairs that stink of charred wood; they are green with moss, and the bannister has gone. I hesitate but only for a second – the sound of our pursuer is getting louder.

'Oi – YOU!' A fierce yell echoes up the stairwell. The stairs stop at a small corridor and another flight of stairs, even more decayed. I look back at the way we've come. My phone light shows up a great hulking shadow. A hand.

I'm neck and neck with Onyx. The stairs end and – we are in a room, but there is something wrong with the floor. It starts okay but then it bends like no floor should do. The carpet's gone. Floorboards are snapped like bust ribs and the whole lot slides into a chasm of blackness.

'We can get across here,' Onyx says, as she steps onto the flat part nearest the wall. 'Look, if we tread carefully, we can get round.'

'It's too dangerous!' I say, one foot on the floor and another beside the wall. 'Onyx don't!' She is just in front of me, picking her way along beside the wall, holding her arms out to the sides to balance. I start to follow, but suddenly the floor creaks and tips further.

'Crap!' She jolts to the side and the torch slips out of her hand.

'Don't move! You can't see.' I fumble to get mine, but the hulk of the man has reached us and Onyx in sheer terror is creaking further away from me. I find the switch and flash it first on Onyx.

The light illuminates her, balanced at the edge of the chasm.

'Onyx! No!' I take a step toward her, but a hand grabs me.

I turn my torch on him. A face, not the face of a monster, just an old face, lined and full of concern.

'Don't carry on!' he calls. 'You'll kill yerself if you fall down there.'

'Onyx, it's okay. Don't panic.'

'I can't move.' Her voice has shrunk. I shine the light toward her, trying not to blind her.

'Get down on your knees and scramble back the way you've come.' I kneel down to show her. She goes down on all fours. I can see tears are starting to glitter on her face.

'You can do it.' I smile at her.

She starts to crawl forwards, hand, knee, hand, knee, and I begin to feel optimistic; the man kneels next to me – I catch a scent of sour must and old beer – holding out a hand to her. She is getting closer, but just before she is in touching distance, there is an enormous CREEEEEEEAAAAAAK and the floor and Onyx disappear down into the blackness.

The sound of Onyx screaming, and the noise of the fall will stay with me forever; a sort of whumping cracking noise, where breakable things meet unforgiving concrete.

'Christ,' the man says, pulling me back from the new edge that is by our knees.

I shine my torch into the empty space. Dust rises in clouds from the mounds of broken wood and plaster, boarding and tile, and among it I can see Onyx's arms and head, still and unmoving.

3.56 A.M.

'We need to ring for an ambulance. You got a phone?' The man asks me.

I nod, unable to speak. My hand shakes as I dial 999. When the woman answers I burst into tears, and the man takes the phone from my hand.

'Ambulance, please,' he says. There's a pause then, 'There's a young kid had an accident. At the old hospital, behind the supermarket in Brynffynnon. Yeah, Denham. It's in the building. She's fallen through the roof. She's not moving.' He listens carefully. 'Which way? Oh right. Yeah. We'll come down and show you. No, just me and the kid's friend. What's your name?' he asks me.

'Mo – Prendergast. And its Ony… Carys Melling. She's twelve.'

'Did you catch that? No, Melling. Okay. See you in a minute.' He hands the phone back to me.

'We need to go meet the ambulance to show them where she is. I thought you were those bloody druggies,' he says, as he begins to tread carefully back to the corridor. I notice he limps slightly. 'But you're not, are you?'

'I can't leave her,' I say, standing rigidly, staring down to where Onyx lies. 'I need to go down to her.'

Onyx could be dead and it's all my fault. It was my stupid idea to come to this place. I encouraged her and now she's lying… I can't bear to think of it, but the image of her still body with the dust is pinned to my eyes.

'Come down and we can see if there's a way to get to 'er without breaking yer neck.' He holds his hand out to beckon me and reluctantly I follow.

I sniff, trying to hold in the storm of feelings inside me.

'That's the only reason I chased you,' he says regretfully. 'I thought you were druggies. Why you in here anyway?' he asks me. There is a sigh in his voice.

'We – I – wanted to explore,' is all I can manage.

'There're signs up fer a reason. This way.' Instead of taking the steps down to the old kitchen, to clamber through the window, he turns right and behind the staircase. There is a small passageway that leads to an old back entrance. There is a catch on the grille that he moves to the side and then easily pushes the metal to one side so we can walk through.

'Are you a security guard?' I ask. Though looking

at the old parka with a rip in the back, the holey gloves and the scent of him, I think not.

'I stay here sometimes. Halloween and Bonfire Night are not good times to be on the street. Here.' He cuts up through the brush and scrub to a muddy track. 'We'll wait for the ambulance.'

'I want to go in and find her,' I say, staring at the brooding building that towers over us.

'Leave it to the experts, kid. They'll know how to get to her without causing more damage. You better ring your folks, don't yer think? I'm guessing they don't know where yer are.'

Fresh tears start to fall again as I think of telling Dad. How they'll never trust me again.

'Everyone makes mistakes,' he says quietly. 'I should know. But that doesn't mean you can run away from them. You're only a kid. Christ, I was up to all sorts when I was your age. Go on, ring 'em.'

The phone rings six times before Dad picks up, his voice fuzzy with sleep.

'Dad, can you come?'

'Mo? You okay?' I hear the bed creak.

'No,' I sniffle. The blue lights of the ambulance are visible behind the high fence. There is the sound of chains being removed. 'There's been an accident. I'm okay, but it's Onyx.'

'Onyx? Carys?'

'Yes. She's hurt. She could be dead.' I start to sob and it's hard to breathe.

'Oh, Mo. Where are you? I'm coming.'

'I'm at th … the old hospital. The ambulance is here.'

'Denham?' There is a pause and he mumbles something I can't hear. 'Okay, Mo. I'm coming. Don't move.' I hear him whispering and the bed creak. 'I'll be there in five minutes, okay, love.' I nod and cry and then the phone goes dead.

4.49 A.M.

A fire engine, ambulance and the police turn up. The old guy shows them where to look. They have massive torches with them, and I am not allowed to go in the building. They enter on the side after removing another grille to gain access.

Then Dad arrives, just as a policewoman starts to ask me questions.

'Oh, Mo.' Dad crushes me to him and I sob into his armpit. 'What's happened? What are you doing here?'

'That's just what I was about to ask Mr… Prendergast?'

'Yes, that's right. Tony, call me Tony.'

They both turn to look at me. I pause, take a deep breath and then tell them.

'And then she just fell. I'd have fallen too if it wasn't for the homeless man holding on to me.' I turn about to see where he's gone, but I can't see him. 'He must be down there with the fire people,' I say.

'Mo, what were you thinking? I told you not to come here. I said it was dangerous.' Dad has his head in his hands. 'We must ring Carys' parents.' He fumbles in his pocket for his phone. 'Have you got their home number, Mo?'

I shake my head.

'I better phone your mum and see if she has a contact number.'

'You can't tell them. Her dad. Her dad will never let me see her again.' I break down.

'We have to tell the next of kin,' the police officer says. 'Do you know the address? I can send a patrol car round.'

'It's a house on the other side of the park – is it Eastside Road? That's right, Mo, isn't it?' Dad says, his arm tight around me.

'Eastside Lane? Yes. What number?' the police officer replies.

I shake my head. 'There's a red door – lions next to the gate.'

'Okay.' The police officer radios through the details, while Dad has a very awful conversation with Mum. She has no number for Carys' home, but is insisting on coming over too. 'Perhaps you should take Mo home?' the police officer suggests, observing me shivering. It isn't the cold though that is making me shake, but the fear – the terrifying thought that Onyx is dead.

'I'm not going until I know she's alright,' I say, shaking off Dad's gentle hand that tries to enclose my arm.

'I'll go and see how things are progressing.' The police officer uses her torch to navigate a way down to the entrance. Bright lights are visible through gaps in the building, and people keep running past with pieces of equipment, shovels and a big foam mat amongst them.

'If I hadn't thought of it, Onyx would be safe at home.' I sniffle.

'I don't think you can take all of the responsibility, Mo.' Dad gives me a sideways hug as we both continue to watch the rescue. 'It sounds like Onyx was more than happy to come along.'

I don't reply, because at that moment, the paramedics appear holding a stretcher. They move swiftly towards us, up the grassy slope and to the waiting ambulance. I can make out a shape strapped down, a human shape, but as I move forward, the doors slam and the ambulance – lights flashing – arrows out of the gate and away.

'She's in a bad way,' says the police officer. 'But she is alive.'

3.15 P.M.

I turn over in bed, wondering why it is so bright outside and why my head aches so badly, but then the memories clatter back into place in my brain as I recall the worst night of my life.

'Hey, sleepy head.' Mum comes in with a cup of milky tea and some biscuits. 'I thought you might like these.'

I nod and scratch my head.

'How did I get here?' The last thing I remember is Mum arriving and walking me up to the road. The police had got hold of Onyx's mum and she was going straight to the hospital.

'Oh, why didn't we go to the hospital?' I say, bolting up and almost spilling the tea in Mum's hand. 'How is Onyx? I've got to go.'

'Hey, hey. Yes, you can go, but not this second, okay? You were in no fit state this morning. You fell asleep in the car so your dad and I brought you here. Onyx has regained consciousness, thank goodness. She's broken her femur – that's her thigh bone – a couple of ribs and her little finger for good measure. She's bruised from head to toe, but there's no obvious brain or nerve damage, so she should heal. She's a very lucky girl.'

I sit back against the pillow and breathe out. 'Thank God.'

'Yes, and thank the brilliant doctors and paramedics that looked after her.'

'And the man.'

'What man?'

'The homeless guy who saved me. If it wasn't for him, it would've taken them hours to find her.' I take a sip of my tea.

'What homeless guy, Mo? I didn't see anyone.'

TUESDAY 2 NOVEMBER

'No Egyptian mummy jokes, okay?' Onyx says when she sees me at the door, my arms laden with sweets, pop and art stuff.

I smile as tears start to form in my eyes. She has a massive plaster on her right leg. 'Not even a little one?' I say.

Onyx's parents are both there. Her mum stands up to greet my mum, who takes her in a hug that seems to last for ages. Onyx's dad is hidden behind a newspaper, that he flicks and folds, placing carefully on the spare chair next to him.

'How on earth did you know which ward Carys was on?' he says standing. 'Nina?' He glares at his wife who sniffs.

'Mo was really worried about Carys,' my mum says. 'She just wanted to see she was okay.'

'Okay?' Mr Melling's face scrunches with rage. 'Does she look okay?'

'I … I'm so, so sorry. I was just interested in the history. I never meant for anyone to get hurt—'

'Well, someone did. My daughter, who, thanks to you, won't be able to walk properly for up to a year!'

'It wasn't Mo's fault,' Onyx says, wincing as she tries to move position.

'Well, whose fault was it?' he says, his voice rising.

'It's okay, Carys,' I say, wanting to protect her from any more harm. 'It was my idea.'

'Well, from now on my daughter will not be seeing you again. She will not be returning to Ysgol Offa and you will not contact her.'

'Dad!' Onyx pleads.

'I'm not sure that is the best decision, Mr Melling,' Mum says, coming to stand beside me and putting her arm around me. 'I agree the girls have been very foolish, but I really think they have learnt their lesson from what's happened here—'

'I'm not interested in your opinion,' Mr Melling says to my mum.

'Dad, you are not stopping me being friends with Mo!' Onyx says, tears seeping from her eyes. 'She's the best thing that's happened to me. It was my idea to go at night. We would never have got into trouble if I hadn't insisted.'

'Well, that just shows her bad influence on you.'

'But I wanted to do something crazy, because you make me feel crazy! Nothing's ever good enough for you. Ever right.' Onyx's face is wet with tears. The room feels so full of tension. I grab hold of Mum's hand – something to keep me anchored. My feet are twitching with anxiety so much I need to balance myself against her.

'You want to change me all the time and you can't – if you stop me seeing Mo, it will make me worse, not better,' Onyx cries.

'ENOUGH!' he roars. 'I want you to leave! Now!' He starts to come toward Mum and me, brushing us away with his arms.

'George.' Mrs Melling's quavering voice pipes up from where she is still standing, pale and small. 'You're upsetting Carys.'

'ME?' roars Mr Melling. 'I'm upsetting her? It wasn't me who led her into a deathtrap!'

A nurse pops her head around the door. 'Is everything okay in here?'

'These people are just going,' Mr Melling spits.

Mum glances to Onyx's mum, but she just has her head bowed as she fiddles with a tissue in her hand.

'Okay, we are leaving,' Mum says, tugging at my hand.

The last thing I hear is Onyx whimpering, 'No,' as Mum pulls me out of the door.

WEDNESDAY 3 NOVEMBER

When Mum drops me at Dad's, they have a long, whispered conversation on the doorstep. I keep hold of my blanket, not caring if Diane looks disapproving, and head indoors.

Stink is in the lounge, sitting on a blanket surrounded by spitty toys. He grins and claps and goes, 'Moh Moh!' when he sees me, which is pretty sweet.

'He's saying your name!' Diane says, and claps. 'Clever Ewan! It's Mo!'

'Hi Ewan,' I say. 'I'm going upstairs,' I tell them, and drag my bag up to my room.

The room smells of polish, which is nice, and there's a little box of chocolates on the pillow. That's not normal, but I'm not complaining. I take one out of its wrapper and stuff it in my mouth. Then I pull out my phone and put it on charge. No messages.

I've heard nothing from Onyx since the hospital visit yesterday. Mum was so cross when we left. She was shouting about how Onyx's dad was an abusive, old-fashioned man and she wasn't going to stand by and let him ruin a young life, but by the time she got home she'd gone quiet. Nev said there wasn't much she could do and that was the end of it.

There is a soft tap on my door.

'Come in.'

Dad is wearing his Christmas polar bear socks that I bought him last year. He shuts the door on Stink's shouting behind him and sits on the edge of my bed.

'How're you doing, my MoMo?' he asks.

I shrug. 'Onyx isn't answering my messages.'

'Maybe her dad isn't allowing her to have her mobile.' He pauses and brushes his neck with his hand. 'Some parents are stricter than others, aren't they?'

'But he is so mean. She's my only friend. He'll never let us be friends anymore.' The tears that have been coming on and off since yesterday start again. I put my blanket on my face.

'Oh, Mo.' Dad strokes my arm gently. 'I'm sure when things settle down you'll be able to talk again. He probably needs time to calm down.'

The doorbell pings. 'Has your mother forgotten something?' Dad stands up. 'I'll be back in a sec.'

I hope we can still be friends. School will be hell if I don't have Onyx. Isn't it bad enough punishment that she got so hurt?

'Mo?' Dad's back, poking his head through the doorway. 'You're going to have to come down.'

'Why?' I sit up and automatically put my blanket under the pillow. 'Who is it?'

'It's nothing to worry about, okay,' he says, with worry gambolling across his face like a flock of terrified sheep, 'but you must come down for a minute. It's the police.'

In the lounge, two police officers are sitting on the big sofa. Diane has picked Stink up and is bouncing him on her hip while he grumbles to be let down.

'Oh, here's Mo now. Tony, I'll take Ewan in the kitchen,' Diane says to Dad. 'Shall we have dindins?' She smiles at Stink as she escapes. I wish I was Stink right now and able to get out of here.

The two people buttoned into their uniforms on our sofa look utterly out of place, all angular and heavy. Both of them have shiny shoes on.

'This is Maureen Prendergast?' the bigger one says.

'Mo,' Dad says, propelling me toward the armchair where he encourages me to sit. He perches on the arm, a barrier between me and the heavies. 'How can we help?'

'We wanted to come and have a little chat, Mo, about your visit the other night to Denham hospital.

Okay? I'm PC Sharpe and this is PC Phillips,' the smaller one says.

I nod my head to the side slightly, still looking at their shoes. I can see the stitching along the sides. There is a bit of mud caught in some of the stitching.

'...often these cases of anti-social behaviour can act as gateway crimes, if not nipped in the bud...' I only realise PC Sharpe's talking when Dad interrupts.

'I think calling it anti-social behaviour is a bit extreme,' Dad says, shuffling forward. 'Mo was desperate to see inside the hospital because she's fascinated by the Victorian health system. She didn't want to cause any damage.'

I look up to watch their faces. PC Sharpe glances at PC Phillips with one of those confusing expressions.

'Whatever you want to call it, Mr Prendergast, breaking and entering private property is dangerous and illegal.' PC Phillips clears his throat. 'Luckily, the owners of the site do not wish to prosecute, despite damage caused. It is our job to have a little chat with the youngsters involved and make sure they realise the severity of what they did. Did you see the "Do Not Enter" signs, Mo?' He directs this to me.

I nod.

The police officer leans back against Diane's best cushions. 'So did you not think those signs meant you?'

There is a pause, then Dad says, 'I'm sure Mo did realise she wasn't supposed to go in there, but I think the pull to find out was too much for her.'

'Is that right, Mo?' PC Sharpe asks.

I nod again. 'I didn't know Onyx was going to hurt herself. I didn't really want to go in the dark because I wanted to be able to see where they kept the people but, well, we ended up going in when it was dark, which was a mistake. I won't go back,' I say. 'She's my best friend and she's hurt and that isn't what was supposed to happen.'

'Onyx? I have a Carys Melling written here,' the bigger one says, looking at his phone.

'She likes to be called Onyx,' I say quietly.

'As you are only twelve and you have not broken the law before, we won't take it any further this time, but if there are any more incidents, then you can be charged and go to court,' PC Phillips states.

'Isn't this a bit over the top?' Dad says, brushing his hand over the top of his head. 'Mo isn't that kind of child, honestly. She doesn't go around the streets with a bottle of vodka in each pocket knocking over old ladies!'

'This is just procedure,' PC Sharpe says, a bit more gently.

'Is the old man okay?' I ask. 'The one that was there

that night. He showed the ambulance people where to find her and helped me out, but then he disappeared.'

'Old man?' The officer looks at his notes, and then at his colleague. 'I've got no notes about a man being there, sorry.'

'Yes he was there. In the building. Dad?' I look to him to help me, but he ruffles my hair distractedly.

'Thank you for your time. There certainly won't be any more incidents,' Dad says. 'Mo's got the message.' He stands up. The police officers also stand.

'One more thing,' PC Phillips says, checking his phone. 'Mr Melling, Carys' father, is insisting that Mo was the instigator. He is talking about seeking legal advice.'

'But as far as we can ascertain, Carys was a willing participant,' PC Sharpe says. 'So, I wouldn't worry.'

When they finally leave, Dad makes a joke of it and we all have tea, but I notice the worry sheep are still gambolling across his face, even at bedtime.

MONDAY 8 NOVEMBER

No message from Onyx. She hasn't even read my last ones. Maybe Dad is right and she isn't allowed her phone. I put my phone away in my bag and make my way up the school drive.

I thought starting secondary school was bad enough in September, but going back today feels even worse. At least I was hopeful then. Now I've lost my best friend and I'm a criminal AND I have Miss Pool to deal with. If it wasn't for the play, I'd run away.

The first people I encounter are Sambhav and Mylo who are desperate to know all the gory details.

'Has Onyx really broken her back?'

'Maya said she'll never walk again!' Mylo sits on my desk swinging his legs.

'No and no,' I say, getting out my planner and batting them away from the desk with it. 'She was in traction, but she's had an operation on her leg. It was her leg that was broken.'

'Move away, you vultures,' Ellie's voice carries across the classroom. 'I'm sure Mo doesn't want to go through it all again. Leave her alone.' She strides towards me and plants herself in the seat next to me.

'I bet she's got a cast. She and I are like twins, yeah? Breaking things.'

I'm thinking that Ellie and Onyx are as much like twins as a tornado and a tomato. 'You've got rid of your big cast.' I nod at the blue wrist support she's wearing.

'I know! It came off over the holidays. The consultant says it's healed really well. I'm back in the gym now. I still can't do weight-bearing stuff for another four weeks, but Coach is confident I'll be competing again soon.' Ellie twists her arm back and forth showing me her brace. 'I could probably even do your part in the play now. You know. If you decide you don't want to do it.'

'But I do,' I say. I watch as Maya and the other wannabes all strut into the class together, just after the bell to make a point.

'Back in a mo, Mo.' Ellie snorts at her own bad joke as she grabs her bag and coat and hurries over to sit next to Maya, just as the form tutor starts calling our names. So, they've made up again. I won't even have Ellie to talk to anymore.

Waiting outside maths, I feel sick. Everyone is subdued until Harry calls, 'Supply!' and everyone starts chattering loudly.

My body feels like the band holding it tight has just snapped. Miss Pool's not in! I'm as happy as an aardvark, as I follow everyone else into the room.

'I bet it's all because of me.' Ellie turns round to me. 'I told my mum.'

'Told your mum what?' I ask suspiciously.

'About how Miss Pool bullies you. She's rung your mum.' She flicks her ponytail. 'It's okay. No need to thank me.'

'What? When?' I ask, but Ellie has disappeared to sit at the back with the wannabes. I sit in my normal place next to Sambhav, just in case it's a trick and Miss Pool appears with her eyebrows of doom. Mum didn't say anything to me. What is Ellie going on about?

When I reach Mum's car at the end of a long, lonely day, instead of turning on the engine she opens her door and gets out.

'What are you doing?' I ask confused.

'We're going to have a little chat with the headteacher,' Mum says, firmly shutting her car door. 'I've spoken to her over the phone about this a couple of times, but we need to clear things up once and for all.'

'What things? Why?' I hurry after her as she steps into the tide of kids escaping school for the day. My mind immediately jumps to the accident. Ban me from history? Mum hasn't said much since the nighttime visit to Denham, but she's been as spiky as a cactus.

'Mum. Why?' I tug at her arm as we reach the entrance to the school reception.

'We need to have a little chat with the headteacher about maths.'

The meeting with the head was excruciating, embarrassing and brilliant!

Mum annihilated Miss Pool.

Ellie told her mum, who told *my* mum, that Miss Pool has been bullying me all term. Mum said, because I am autistic, teachers have to make reasonable adjustments in class. Apparently sending me out for every lesson doesn't count! Mum said I fidget because it's a stim and she said I need extra processing time.

Mrs Flax apologised five times! I counted. She said that not all teachers were as aware of my needs as they should be. She said she would, 'work with my teachers to ensure they meet my needs more effectively.' Ha!

At bedtime, Mum peeks round my door to see if I want the light turning off. I'm just finishing reading a library book called *Cholera: The Victorian Plague*, which I can't put down.

'MoMo?'

'Mmm?'

She comes in and sits on the edge of my bed, putting a hand to my hair and stroking a strand behind my ear.

'I wish you'd told me how awful that maths teacher was being to you. I know Ellie's a pain, but if it wasn't for her, I would never have known.'

I scrunch my eyes shut.

'It must have been so horrible. It makes me feel so sad knowing you were going through that and felt you couldn't tell me or your dad.'

I breathe in and hold my breath, wriggling my toes in the bed. Her hand is gently stroking my hair.

'I'm not cross with you, darling. I wonder how we can help you communicate the difficult things, though.'

I don't know what to say. I breathe out. I don't want my mum to be sad, but I know I can't speak when the feelings get too big. It's like they squash the words out of me and there's no room left. Onyx floats into my head. When we were stuck in Denham. She'd said we were together and that it would all be okay. Instead of saying that though I say, 'Soursticks.'

'If it's bad again that could be the code word? Soursticks? You would just need to tell me the code word and I'll know.'

'But I like soursticks,' I say, snuggling up next to her.

'You hate—'

'—Brussels sprouts!' we both say, laughing.

'Okay. If things get bad again in maths – if she sends you out, or doesn't give you enough time to finish, or shouts at you for wriggling your feet, or anything else that makes you feel bad, you just need to tell me "Brussels sprouts", and I'll sort it.' She hugs me and I nod.

'Shall we have one last go at practising your lines before tomorrow's rehearsals?'

And so, we do.

WEDNESDAY 10 NOVEMBER

I'm rushing down the corridor towards the hall at the end of the day for rehearsals, when Lara catches up with me.

'Hey, little bug, how you doing? Whole cast run through tonight!' They grin. They are wearing a baggy black hoodie with a picture of a possum on it playing the guitar. 'I heard about your adventure at the old hospital.' They pause beside the double doors.

'Oh.' I look down at my feet embarrassed. 'Yeah. Not the best idea we ever had.'

They shrug. 'Sometimes we do these things. I'm glad your friend is okay though. Onyx, right?'

'I think she's okay. I'm not allowed to speak to her anymore.'

'Oh no!' Lara looks genuinely concerned. 'Your little buddy. Why?'

'Her dad blames me. He's got weird ideas anyway about … about … well, he's just really old fashioned. He says he's going to make her move schools.'

'That's cruel. Even if it was your idea, I'm sure you didn't force her. You aren't that kind of person.'

'No, she wanted to go, and it was her idea to go at night,' I explain. 'I just wanted to see it for myself. Did you know they used to put people there who didn't fit: autistics, gay people, anyone who society didn't think was normal? I wanted to see it. See if I could make sense of it, but – well...' I pause, surprised I've said so much. They are listening, watching me. 'Well, it was just cold and wet and we got stuck in there, then someone followed us and Onyx fell.'

Lara hesitates for a moment, then says, 'Things aren't like that now. That's what you've got to remember. You can be yourself and be accepted.'

'Yeah, but Onyx can't,' I mutter, peering through the glass of the door. The hall is busy. Chairs are laid out, all facing the stage. The girl playing Billy Whizz is standing talking to Lydia Matek. Ellie, Chantelle and Soraya are up on the stage practising their dancing. Harry and Sambhav are wrapping themselves up in the giant curtains tied at the edge of the stage.

'Is Onyx not allowed to be herself?' Lara moves away from the door and leans against the wall. 'You know we run an LGBTQ+ group here at school? Some people are still so bigoted, but everyone has a right to be themselves. It's a nice group. Maybe Onyx can come when she's better? If she's, you know, interested.'

I risk a glance at their face and their expression is kind. 'If I ever get to speak to her again, I'll tell her,' I say.

'You will,' they say, grabbing me in a bone-crushing hug. 'Always here if you need to chat, little bug.' They push the door open with a Barnabas flourish. 'Come on. Let's do this!'

MONDAY 15 NOVEMBER

It's 9:01 a.m. and there's no sign of her. That makes it thirteen days since I've seen or heard from Onyx. Every day feels so lonely. The only person who really speaks to me is the librarian. I'm even missing Ellie annoying me!

We're lining up outside maths and something feels different. The table outside Miss Pool's room – *my* table – has gone and someone's tacked a poster on the door. It's a picture of Einstein with a quote: *A person who never made a mistake, never tried anything new.*

Ellie pokes her nose in the classroom and raises her eyebrows. 'Who's that?'

'Ooh, dunno,' Soraya says, making a shocked face. 'No Miss Pool again though! Probably another supply teacher.'

We all trudge in. I choose a seat at the back away from everyone.

A teacher with straight shiny hair and glasses stands in front of the whiteboard. 'Good day, year seven. My name is Ms Williams. I'm going to be teaching you maths for the rest of this term. Now, can you tell me where your books are kept?' Hands fly up and whispers flutter about the room.

'Ms Williams, where's Miss Pool?' Maya asks.

'I'm afraid Miss Pool has decided to take early retirement. I will look after you, though. Now the books?'

I'm too amazed to speak. Miss Pool has gone from my life forever!

FRIDAY 19 NOVEMBER

The bell goes to pack up from history and I'm just walking out of the door when Mr Brock calls me back. I've never stood too near him before. He smells sort of lemony and I notice that his beard has ginger, brown and white hairs all tangled together.

'Hello, Mo.' Mr Brock's mouth smiles, but I can't see his eyes as his glasses reflect the strip-light glare of the classroom. 'I believe you met my wife, Margaret. She works at the library. She told me she'd met a remarkable young person who was fascinated by local history. Then when I heard what happened over half term, I put two and two together.'

I nod.

'She told me you'd been looking through the old registers of the hospital.' He sits back on his stool. 'I do have a certain sympathy for you. For wanting to find out about history firsthand.' He clears his throat. 'But there are – safer ways to go about it. So—'

'My great uncle was in Denham,' I explain,

thinking he might actually be interested. A teacher who is interested – rare as a rhino in a raincoat!

'Really! Well, Margaret and I got to thinking, and I'm going to start up a history society here at the school, one lunchtime. We thought you might like to come. And, if people are interested, we could maybe do the odd visit or two, to local places of interest. Safely, of course.' He grins at me. 'What do you think?'

I smile. Somewhere else to go apart from the library!

WEDNESDAY 24 NOVEMBER

Onyx has seen my messages! The little icon that shows they've been read is highlighted at last. I send another:

Still missing you. Hope you can come back to school soon.

I stare at my phone hoping for a reply until I get told by the form tutor to put my phone away.

Today we are having our first dress rehearsal and I head over to the classrooms near the hall to get changed. Maya and the wannabes are hanging about again. They keep coming with Ellie and waiting outside while we're rehearsing, looking through the big windows and making loads of noise which is really annoying. I can see some of them in the doorway chatting as I walk over the quad.

They're stood in front of the doors and ignore me as I reach them.

''Scuse me,' I say politely.

'Thinks she's special now,' Maya says, without moving out of my way. A wannabe snorts with laughter. 'Special little role for a special little freak.'

Just then Ellie bursts through the door. 'Coming through, coming through!' Ellie calls loudly. She's hanging on the arm of one of the year nine boys who helps with the lighting.

'Oh, hi Mo.' She grins at me. 'Hope you girls are playing nice. Maya, this is Jake.'

Maya flicks her hair over her shoulder as she looks him over.

'Any problems, Mo, let me know. 'Kay?' Ellie holds the door open for me, as I scurry through saying nothing. It seems even though she's back with her old friends, she's not going back to being a complete bitchington. Well, there are miracles.

I head for the classroom where the girls are getting changed. The choir are here, too, even though they are only wearing red T-shirts and black leggings. They are crowded in around the tables chatting noisily. I hate getting changed in front of other people. It's like in PE where we are all expected to get our clothes off in front of each other, packed in like biscuits. I find a spot near the wall and put my stuff down. Ms Latimer hands me my costumes.

'The brown skirt and white blouse are for act one: scene three, only. You have a quick change to do, while they move the scenery round and you put the unitard on. You need make-up for your beard too, once you've changed. We'll practise the timings today, okay?' Ms Latimer smiles, then moves on to hand out more costumes.

I hold up the red glittering thing with sequins up one side. It's like a leotard with arms and legs.

'I wish my dress was red,' Ellie complains loudly, as she enters the classroom. She barges in beside me, wriggling out of her T-shirt, proudly displaying her bra. 'I hate purple.' She grabs her dress and shakes it.

'I love purple,' Lydia Matek says. She plays one of the main parts, Rosemary.

I'm not really concentrating, mainly because I'm too busy wondering how the hell I'm going to get into the full-length bodysuit. 'I'm just going to the toilet,' I say finally, scurrying out into the quiet part of the school to find a cubicle to hide in.

I slam the toilet door shut and slip the latch across. I can still hear the excited chatter, but it is distant, and I have room to breathe. What am I going to do? I haven't worn a leotard since I quit gymnastics nearly three months ago, and this thing is a full-body one with arms and legs. In that time, I've sprouted blubbery boobs that hang about on my chest like anaemic anemones.

I drag the stupid costume on over my bottom half. Leaving my T-shirt on, I try to pull the top part up, but the T-shirt gets rucked up. It makes it look like I have some kind of rippling alien stomach system, as well as sticking out round my neck in an itchy way.

Pulling the top of the leotard down, I yank the T-shirt off, hurting my neck in the process. I force my arms back into the leotard and ping it into place. It fits perfectly. Smooth and snug across all parts of my body. My breasts blare at the front, poking out the material in little humps. I cross my arms over my chest and push them down, but they boing back again. Stupid puberty. Stupid body. Stupid costume. I yank the whole thing off. It catches on my feet, and I rip at it getting more and more angry until I'm free of it. It lies on the floor like a dead skin. I pull at my hair in frustration.

The door to the bathroom opens gently. 'Mo?'

It's Ms Latimer.

I hold my breath for a moment, but it's pointless, my clothes have spilled out under the cubicle door. It's obvious I'm here.

'Yeah. I won't be long,' I say, trying to make my voice sound steady. If I can get her to go away, I'll ring Dad to fetch me, and they can let Ellie have the part. She'll be brilliant at all this showing off. But Ms Latimer doesn't go away, instead she comes to the outside of the cubicle.

'Do you want to talk? Is it the costume?'

I nod. Even though she can't see it. I nod and a tear sneaks its way down my nose.

'I don't mind if you don't want to wear it today. It's more important you get used to doing the run through. You are a brilliant little actor. That's what matters.'

I sniff. 'How did you know? About the costume?'

'I saw your look of absolute terror when I gave it to you. I sort of guessed. I know you have some sensory issues so when you didn't come back from the toilet, I guessed you might be struggling. Wear your normal clothes. Okay?'

I sniff and nod again. 'Okay.'

I hear the door shut behind her and breathe out. Changing back into my uniform, I try to bring all the bits of myself back together, ready to go on the stage and be Clara, the bearded lady.

MONDAY 29 NOVEMBER

Not long until the play now. I'm dreading it. School is Offal without you.

I press send, hoping she remembers our bad joke about the school. She isn't reading them, but it makes me feel better sending them and it takes my mind off Mum's new mission. We're in Sarah Jane's department store in town and Mum keeps picking up frilly lacy bras and sticking them in my face.

'No,' I say for the hundredth time. She puts it back on the rail a bit more forcefully than she meant to and a few of the stupid bras flutter to the ground like dead butterflies.

She is trying to keep her temper, but she's checked her watch twice and I know the shop shuts at 5.30.

'Help me out here, Mo,' Mum says with exasperation. 'You say you want to cover up, but you don't like anything!'

'I just don't want them,' I hiss at her, not wanting to talk loudly in case people hear. 'I don't want to buy a stupid *bra* at all.'

'This store will be closing in ten minutes. Please take your items to the checkouts. This store will be closing in ten minutes.'

'Oh, for God's sake. Come on then,' Mum snaps at last and stomps out of the shop to the car. I follow her, walking two or three paces behind, a sense of satisfaction rising like swamp mud.

She slams the car door and sits waiting for me. I take a moment or two, then sidle in next to her and shut my door.

'What can I do, Mo?' She looks at me with a sad face now.

I shrug.

There is a pause, then she says, 'Do you think you … you might be like Onyx? Might not like being a girl?'

I put my blanket on my face and close my eyes.

'I mean, if you are, you know Dad and I don't mind. We love you as you are.' I feel her put her hand on my arm gently. 'I'm sorry I was cross in the shop.'

'I didn't mind being me before, being a girl or whatever. It was fine. I just don't like having boobs or pubes! Ugh.' I pull the blanket off my face. 'I mean what's the point in boobs? They just get in the way!'

'Well, if you ever have children, they're important if you want to breastfeed and they're an erogenous zone—'

‘Ugh. Mum!’ I put my hands up to my ears, until she stops talking. ‘It just feels too different. I feel like an alien growing tentacles.’

‘They don’t look like tentacles,’ she says gently.

That makes me laugh. ‘I know they don’t! That’s not the point.’

‘Look,’ Mum says getting her phone out. ‘Maybe a sports bra might suit you better. I prefer them. They feel nice and snug. You can get different colours too. Look on the app.’ She shows me a shopping app and types in the search. ‘You can try them on at home too. It might make you feel less stressed. Okay?’

‘Okay,’ I agree and start scrolling through all the different colours and styles as she drives us home.

TUESDAY 30 NOVEMBER

Nev's just come back with a takeaway and Mum's putting it all on plates. It smells gorgeous.

'That plate's mine,' I say, eyeing the one with the biggest spareribs.

'I should get the most,' Nev says in mock shock. 'I went to fetch it after all!'

'Mo can choose. She needs cheering up,' Mum says, as she carries the plates over to the table. 'So do you want to tell her or shall I?'

'Tell me what?'

'You tell her.' Nev grins, poking a spring roll with his fork.

'We know you are fed up at the moment, missing Onyx and after everything, well, we thought that at the weekend we could go to Scapmoor Park!'

'Really?' I've been asking to go to Scapmoor for years. It's the best theme park in the country. 'But isn't it hours away?' I take a bite of one of my ribs. 'You said we couldn't do it in a day.'

'That's why we're going to drive up on Saturday

and stay over. Special treat.' Mum looks all happy and I don't want to say I don't want to go, but I don't. I just want Onyx back. I try to look pleased.

'Thanks, I was going to ask whether we could call in on Onyx and see how she is? Can we do that before we go? I know I'm not supposed to talk to her, but maybe Onyx's mum would speak to you?'

Nev glances at Mum.

'I don't think we can.'

'Why? What's happened?'

'I got hold of Onyx's mum's mobile the night of the accident. Her name's Nina. I've texted her a few times.' Mum puts her knife and fork down. 'She doesn't always answer. I think her husband is quite controlling. Well, after the way he behaved in the hospital I sent her a message. I thought it was wrong the way he spoke about Onyx, and I was worried about Nina – well, she doesn't stand up for herself at all, does she?'

'Your mum told Nina she's living with an emotionally abusive man and she should leave him, basically. That's what you said!' Nev adds.

'Not quite in those words,' Mum replies frowning.

'What happened?' I say.

'She didn't reply.' Mum looks down.

'Oh, Mum! You could've found out how Onyx was.'

'She didn't reply until this afternoon.' Mum glances at Nev, then at me. 'Nina's left him. She and Onyx have moved to Onyx's aunt's house. Nina's getting a divorce.'

I jump out of my seat and clap my hands. 'That's great! Onyx can be who she wants to be now. She doesn't have to pretend. And we can be friends again!'

'Sort of,' Mum says, looking down again.

'What? What aren't you telling me?'

'Onyx's aunt lives in Birmingham.'

WEDNESDAY 8 DECEMBER

I hitch the leotard on, pulling it here and there to make sure it's comfy. Mum was right, I much prefer sports bras. I've got my new one on that came yesterday. It's green and soft and I like how it feels, like a band across my chest.

Ms Latimer let me take my costume home so I could get used to it. Mum cut the label out and now I'm almost happy. Almost. I'm still getting changed in the toilet, but that's okay.

I put on the brown skirt and white blouse over the top of the leotard – it's the only way I can do the change between scenes in time, then I go out to the wings. We are learning to stand now so we can get our exits and our entrances organised.

Charlie wanders toward the stage from the boy's changing area. He's wearing clown trousers and a wig and humming his song. 'Are you nervous, Mo?'

I make an 'ahhhhhhh' face at him and he laughs. 'Least you don't have to wear an actual beard.' He nods to my face and the brown streaks drawn over my chin in make-up.

'Can you imagine when I'm cartwheeling?' I say, miming a beard over my eyes.

'We're putting the dances in today, aren't we?' Ifan says, appearing on the wings. 'Dancing is not my strong point!'

I nod. 'And the songs.' I watch as Mr Kaspar, the music teacher starts to herd all the chorus into their corner of the stage. Mr Kaspar has given me a bit of voice coaching and they've shortened my song, so I only have one verse on my own, then the chorus join in – and drown me out. But I still sound like an anxious lettuce on a rollercoaster.

The dress rehearsal is going really well until my first scene. I'm on stage on my own, with a low light on me. I have to sit on this piece of scenery – it's like a giant box. I sing the first verse and then I'm supposed to jump down from the box and do cartwheels and flips, while the chorus sing with me, and my mic's turned down.

I'm on the box. The lighting's perfect. My costume isn't annoying me. The music starts. I take a breath, like Mr Kaspar told me, listening for the beat when I start to sing,

'Somebodies are somebody
Somebodies who can be someone
But this one is a nobody
A freak who—'

'Stop! Stop!' Mr Kaspar shouts. I can't really see him with the bright light in my face, but I know he's in front of the stage where the band is. 'Sorry, Mo, that's a bit too quiet. Let's try again. Louder please.'

I end up having to do it three times before he's happy with it. How will I ever get it right on the actual real-live performance?

I stomp off stage at the end, avoiding Lara and Ms Latimer, who are always trying to make me feel better, and head to get changed. But the first thing I do when I close the door is take out my phone.

ONYX!!! Mum says you've left your dad.

Pls message me

Onyx

Onyx

Message MEEEEEEEEE

Are you okay???

I is worried now

Pls

Are you really in Brum?

Is there no signal in Brum?
Are you coming back?
ONYX

Still no reply.

I thought that after Onyx and her mum left her dad, she would be able to text me again, but nothing. Even Nina has stopped texting Mum. Mum tried calling her, but no one picked up. What is going on? Will I ever see her again?

FRIDAY 17 DECEMBER

Sambhav keeps opening the edge of the curtain and peeking through. I can see Mum and Nev, Diane, Dad and Stink on the front row. This is opening night, and my whole brain is required to remember my lines, my actions and especially how to sing.

'Remember you can do this,' Ms Latimer says to us all, 'and that you are all amazing.' She smiles at us as the curtains open and then I don't even have time to worry about worrying because the band is starting. Lara winks at me and steps onto the stage. The show has begun.

'But Mr Barnabas! Mr Barnabas. You promised us.' I pause, letting the tension build. I can't see the audience really, only the brightness of the spotlight. I can almost imagine it is a rehearsal and that lets me focus on my performance. I am Clara.

'We put our trust in you and this, this is how you repay us?' I walk toward Barnabas, who is turned away from me. I let my voice drop with sorrow as I lay my hand on his shoulder. 'You pulled us out of the gutter for what? To throw us back again?'

Barnabas puts his head in his hands.

'What about Molly-Mae? What about Sid? Beans? You expect us to go back? Pretend like this never happened? We can't unknow what you've given us. You've given us hope. Don't take that away from us.'

That is the cue for the rest of the cast to start to sing:

'On freedom's side
So many years we've been denied
The world has robbed us of our pride
But now we stand
On freedom's side!'

At the end of the performance, we all go back on the stage to take a bow together. The lights are up and I can see the audience for the first time. Everyone is cheering and clapping and some people are even standing up. I feel shy, after not even thinking about all those eyes on me, suddenly I want to be invisible. I push slightly back from where I'm supposed to stand. Ellie and Sambhav are more than happy to dodge in front of me.

It is at that moment, when I take a step back, that I notice. Someone at the edge of a row. Someone with crutches leaning against their chair. Someone waving and clapping and grinning at me like a cat whose sniffed all the catnip. It's Onyx.

As soon as I've changed, I charge into the foyer where all the audience are gathering, some putting coats on and others buying drinks and food from the stalls. Did I imagine her?

People stop and pat me on the shoulder, and say well done. Other kids I don't even know smile at me. Mum, Dad, Nev, Diane, even Stink are around me, saying words I can't register. I'm looking for someone and suddenly there she is. Onyx with a crutch under one arm and her mum linking her other arm.

'Mo! You were so amazing!' Onyx says, hobbling over to me, releasing her mum and giving me a one-armed hug.

I can't speak because suddenly my eyes are being weird and watering everywhere. 'I even have weird eyes!' I say, as I sniff and we pull apart.

'I love your weird.' Onyx grins at me, still holding on to me.

'You're here!' Is all I can manage.

'It's a long story,' Onyx says, looking at her mum. 'But we're back now, that's what matters, and I'll be back to school after Christmas.'

My insides feel like a party popper of happiness has just gone off. I can't talk, I'm just so full of grins.

'Shall we get a seat?' Mum says, pointing at a table near the ice cream and drinks stands. 'I'm guessing Onyx might fall over if she has to stand up too long?'

'Good plan,' Onyx's mum, Nina, says, taking Onyx's crutch as she settles into a seat. 'And from now on, Onyx would like to use the they/them pronouns.'

Nina hugs Onyx, who closes their eyes for a long moment.

'Ice cream, anyone?' Dad asks.

It probably sounds like an exaggeration, but I think tonight has been one of the best moments of my life, just sitting all together, eating those ice creams and drinking and chatting, until the caretaker was frowning at us to put the chairs and tables away.

All my family were there, being their own weird and wonderful selves: Onyx, their mum, even Lara and their folks and Ms Latimer sat with us for a bit. It was like a great big chattering bunch of kindness. I didn't say much, I just listened, and that was okay. No one minded. No one made me feel like I was wrong.

I don't know what I will be in the future. I don't know if I'm going to be an actor or a historian, or something else entirely. I don't know if I'll turn out gay or straight or something else. Right now, I feel I can cope with my changing body, the whole topsy turnip of life. Right now, I feel like I love my weird too, and I can't wait for the next chapter.

ACKNOWLEDGEMENTS

I have met many courageous, resilient and witty students in my time. Thank you to every one of you for what you have taught me about being yourselves and using your voices; keep being full-hearted about life.

Special thanks to the gifted Ursula Rowe for being my sensitivity reader. To Victoria Pici, Claire Fayers and the other SCBWIs for their encouragement, brilliant knowledge and advice about stories and audience. Thanks to the Pen-pushers gang: Mary, Jean, Helen, Gill and Jayne for all your help over the years. Thanks to my family and friends for loving my weird.

Thank you to the wonderful Fireflies that make this book magic happen: Penny, Janet and the crew; to the talented Becka Moor and Veronica Carratello for the brilliant cover. Thanks to Hayley Fairhead for her patience and sense when editing this book. Thanks to Graeme and the Bounce marketing team for bouncing it about!

Lastly, thanks to my teachers. Those good ones who saw me and cared and made all the difference.

Chloë Heuch is a neurodivergent author, writer and educator. She has written all her life: poetry, journalling, short stories and even scripts. In 2021 she was shortlisted for the Rhys Davies Short Story Competition and published by Parthian Press. Her YA debut novel *Too Dark to See* came out in 2020 with Firefly Press.

She teaches English part-time at Ysgol Friars secondary school in Bangor. She lives in North Wales with her family. When she's not reading and writing, she can usually be found wandering about the mountains of North Wales with her cocker spaniel and her rather adventurous cat.